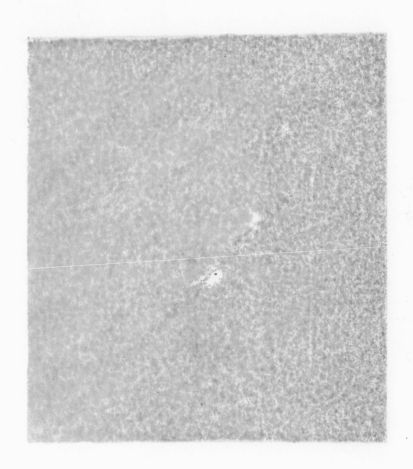

Pearl
IN THE
Egg

Pearl

IN THE

Egg

A TALE
OF THE THIRTEENTH CENTURY

BY

DOROTHY VAN WOERKOM

ILLUSTRATIONS BY JOE LASKER

THOMAS Y. CROWELL / NEW YORK

"The Wandering Song" adapted from "The Princess's Holiday"
by Nora Perry, 1884.

"Bright Morn Breaking" adapted from "An Easter Processional"
by Helen Gray Cone, 1891.

"The Derby Ram" adapted from "The Derby Ram"
by Rosa S. Allen, 1899.

"The Winter Song" adapted from "Listening"
by Mary N. Prescott, 1876.

Pearl in the Egg: A Tale of the Thirteenth Century

Text copyright © 1980 by Dorothy Van Woerkom
Illustrations copyright © 1980 by Joe Lasker

Designed by Al Cetta

Library of Congress Cataloging in Publication Data

Van Woerkom, Dorothy
  Pearl in the Egg.

  SUMMARY: Upon joining a troupe of minstrels who roam the countryside of 13th-century England, young Pearl discovers how much she loves to sing.
  [1. Minstrels—Fiction.   2.   England—Fiction]
  I.   Lasker, Joe.   II.   Title
  PZ7.V39Pe   [Fic]   79–8040
  ISBN 0–690–04029–6
  ISBN 0–690–04030–X (lib. bdg.)
          1 2 3 4 5 6 7 8 9 10
               First Edition

To Elizabeth M. Graves

About the harp used in this story:

"One of the most graceful of ancient instruments is an old boat-shaped harp of Burmah. The body is of dark wood, with a sounding-board of buffalo-hide, and a cluster of silk cords and tassels is a pretty decoration fastened to the curved neck and falling around the front. There are thirteen silk strings, which are tuned by pushing them up and down the neck, to which they are fastened. The player holds the harp on his knee, with its neck over his left arm, and sweeps the strings with his right hand. This beautiful instrument was used only as an accompaniment for songs."
(Quoted from "Some Ancient Musical Instruments" by H. S. Conant, *St. Nicholas* Magazine, May, 1891)

In about 1929 one of these boat-shaped harps, repainted in black and gold, with gold braid and sequins, was presented to the New York City Metropolitan Museum of Art. It is still on display there, in the Musical Instruments Gallery.

AUTHOR'S NOTE

PEARL IN THE EGG and MATILL MAKEJOYE were real people who lived in England in the thirteenth century. They were both minstrels in the court of King Edward I, for their names are so listed in the king's account books. Other than this brief mention, they appear to be lost to history.

I wondered how it was that these thirteenth-century women had taken up the minstrel's life, a life traditionally portrayed in story and picture as a male occupation. I learned that most minstrels *were* men, but that there were some women minstrels as well. They are rarely mentioned in records of the times, and storytellers seem to have overlooked them completely.

Family surnames were only just coming into use in the thirteenth century. Most of the common folk still gave themselves, or were given, names descriptive of their work, or of some physical characteristic, or even of their temperament. So I wondered how Pearl came to have her unusual name.

This story, then, is a story of what might have happened. In writing it I have tried to reconstruct as faithfully as possible the way life was for the children of the poor in those days. If most of the characters seem young by today's reckoning, it is because in those days people reached middle age in their twenties.

CONTENTS

[ix]

CONTENTS

Pearl
IN THE
Egg

ONE

THE HUNT

PEARL set the bowl of cabbage soup down on the floor near the rushlight. She knelt beside the box of straw that was her father's bed. She wiped his forehead, listening to his heavy breathing.

"Please, Fa," she coaxed. She broke off a piece from a loaf of black bread and dipped it into the soup. She placed it on his lips, letting the soup trickle into his mouth. She ate the chunk of bread, and dipped another.

"I will be in the fields until the nooning," she said, "so you must try to eat a little now. See, I have even put a bit of dripping in the soup."

She forced the warm, mild liquid down his throat until the bowl was half empty. She drank the rest herself, chewing hungrily on the lump of fat that the sick man had not been able to swallow.

Again she wiped his face, and then she blew out the light.

She crossed the smooth dirt floor, and pulled a sack from a peg on the wall near the door as she left the hut. Outside, the sky was gray with the dawn. Ground fog swirled around her feet. The air smelled of ripening grain and moist earth.

From other huts of mud and timber, serfs hurried out into the early morning mist. Some, like Pearl, would spend the day in their own small holdings in the fields. It was the time for harvesting their crops, which would feed their families through the winter. Others, like Pearl's older brother, Gavin, had already left for work in the manor fields to bring in Sir Geoffrey's crops.

Sir Geoffrey was lord of the manor, which included his great stone house and all the land surrounding it. He owned this tiny village. He even owned most of the people in it. A few, like the baker, the miller, and the soapmaker, were freemen and free women. They worked for themselves and paid the lord taxes. For tax, Sir Geoffrey collected a portion of everything they produced. No one in the village had money.

But the serfs were not free. They could never leave the manor, or marry without the lord's permission. They could not fish in the streams or hunt in the forest. They owned only their mud huts and small gardens, called holdings, and an ox or cow, or a few geese or sheep. The serfs also paid taxes. Each year they gave Sir Geoffrey a portion of their crops. He took a share of their eggs; if a flock of sheep or geese increased, he took a share; and if a cow had a calf, he took that also. On certain days of the week each family had to send a man—and an ox if they had one—to help plow the lord's fields, harvest his crops, and do other work. Each woman had to weave one garment a year for the lord and his family.

The sun was up when Pearl reached the long furrows of her

field, where the flat green bean pods weighed down their low bushes. She bent to see if the leaves were dry. Wet leaves would wither when she touched them.

The sun had dried them. Pearl began filling her sack, wondering how she could finish the harvest all by herself before the first frost. She had other plots to work as well.

Now that their father was ill, twelve-year-old Gavin was taking his place for three days each week in the manor fields. Sir Geoffrey would get *his* crops safely in! But if the frost came early, or if the only one left at home to work was an eleven-year-old like Pearl, that was of small matter to Sir Geoffrey.

Pearl stood up to rub her back. A serf's life was a hard life. Her father's was, and his father's before him. She sighed. Who could hope to change it?

Old Clotilde came swaying up the narrow path between her field and Pearl's. She waved her empty sack by way of greeting and squatted down among her plants.

"How be your Fa this morning?" she asked Pearl.

"He took some soup. But he wanders in his head. He thinks I am my mother, though she's been dead three summers now."

"Ah, and he'll join her soon, Big Rollin will." Clotilde's wrinkled face was nearly the same dirty gray as her cap. "They all do, soon as they take a mite of sickness. For the likes of us to stay alive, we must stay well! Get the priest for him! He won't plow these fields again."

Before Pearl could reply, the shrill blare of a hunting horn sounded across the meadow, followed by the baying of hounds on the trail of a wild boar. Startled to their feet, the serfs watched the terrified boar running in and out among the rows of crops.

"Run, lest you get trampled!" Clotilde screamed, dashing down

the path toward the forest. The others followed her. Someone pulled Pearl along as she stumbled forward, blinded by angry tears, her fingers tightly gripping her sack.

The hounds came running in pursuit of the boar. Behind the hounds rode the hunting party of twenty horsemen, led by Sir Geoffrey. At the rear was another man Pearl recognized. Jack, one of Sir Geoffrey's bowmen, had come upon her one day as she scrounged for dead branches near the edge of the forest. He had baited her with cruel words, rudely ruffling her hair with the shaft end of an arrow.

"Jack's my name. What's yours?" he had demanded, taking pleasure in her discomfort. For answer she had spat at him, and he had pressed the arrow's metal tip against her wrist until she'd dropped her bundle. Laughing, he had scattered the branches with his foot and grabbed her hair.

"Spit at me again, girl, and that will be the end of you!" Though his mouth had turned up in a grin, his eyes had been bright with anger. His fingers had tightened on the nape of her neck, bending her head back. She had stared up at him, frightened but defiant.

"Perhaps you need a lesson in manners right now," he'd said, raising his other hand. He probably would have struck her, but for the rattle of a wagon and the tuneless whistle signaling someone's approach. He had let her go with a suddenness that had left her off balance, and had stalked away.

Shaken, Pearl had turned to see Sir Geoffrey's woodcutter driving out of the forest with a wagonload of wood for the manor house.

Now Pearl shuddered at the memory; but Jack was taking no notice of her. His eyes were on the boar and on his master.

If the boar became maddened during the chase and turned on one of the hunters, Jack was ready with his arrows to put an end to the beast.

Over the meadow they galloped, and onto the fields. They churned up the soft earth, trampled down the precious bean plants, crushed the near-ripe ears of the barley and oats, tore up the tender pea vines. They chased the boar across the fields and back again, laughing at the sport.

When they had gone, Pearl ran back to her field. She crawled in the turned-up earth, searching for unbroken bean pods. The other serfs were doing the same.

"What is the matter with us?" she demanded of Clotilde. "Why do we stay silent, with spoiled crops all around us, just so Sir Geoffrey will have his sport?"

"Shush!" Clotilde warned, looking quickly around to see who might have heard. "Do you want a flogging for such bold words? Hold your tongue, as you see your elders do."

For the rest of the morning they worked in silence. At midday, Pearl picked up her half-filled sack. It should have been full by now. She glared fiercely across the meadow at the manor house, but she held her tongue.

Pearl returned home to find that her father had worsened. When she could not rouse him, she went for the priest.

"He won't trouble you much longer," Father Alwyn said. His tall, lean body bent low as he dipped a sprig of boxwood into a leather vial and sprinkled the holy water over the dying man. He held up a cross of blessed palm, praying aloud as he moved it over the still form.

"What will become of us, Father?" Pearl whispered.

The priest straightened up. "How old is your brother? By law the house and holdings will be his. But Sir Geoffrey will take your ox as a death due. You know the law."

She flinched. Yet she did know the law. When a man died, his lord took his most valuable possession as a death due.

"Gavin is but twelve," she told him, "though he does the work of a man grown."

The priest shook his head. "Not of proper age. Sir Geoffrey will no doubt give the holdings to someone else. He'll find other use for a strong boy like Gavin."

"And me?" Her voice was shrill. "What of me?"

Father Alwyn shrugged. "Who can say? Sir Geoffrey may send you to a convent to work for the nuns. Or he may bring you to the manor house to work."

"He won't take me away from Gavin?"

"You'll have no say in the matter," the priest said gently, "so try not to bring trouble on yourself." He opened the door. "When the end comes you must tell me at once, so I can report to Sir Geoffrey. It's the law."

Pearl stood in the doorway watching the priest's long legs take him out of sight. Wearily she reached for her sack again, and went to work in the field until sundown.

TWO

A SECRET

IN THE early evening when Pearl came home, she opened the door to rushlight's glow. Gavin was there, kneeling on the floor beside their father. She slammed the door shut behind her and caught her breath. Fa's body was completely hidden, now, beneath a rough blanket.

"He's dead!"

Gavin stood up. "Aye. Stay with him whilst I tell Father Alwyn. The horn will soon blow for curfew."

"Nay, Gavin!" She knelt on the floor, pulling him back down beside her, and told him what the priest had said.

For a long time Gavin stared into the rushlight, thinking. "We'd best go away from here," he said finally.

She blinked. "Where? How would we live?"

"I don't know. But if we get to a town and stay for a year and a day, the law says we'll be free! I have heard folk talk of this."

Pearl considered this. "The village road leads to a town," she said doubtfully, "or so folk say." They had never been farther away from their village than the manor house. "But Sir Geoffrey will surely look for us along that way. What of the woodcutter's track through the forest?"

Gavin got to his feet again. "The forest way is safest. We can hide there for a while, if need be. But we dare not take the track where it enters the woods. Someone may see us. We'll have to cross the fields, then make our way through the trees till we reach it. Somehow we'll get to the other side of the forest and find a town. Come on, we must hurry!"

Pearl had been thinking. "Wait!" she said. "We need time to get food to take with us. Tomorrow you must go to work, just as if it be an ordinary day. I'll take flour to Faxon Baker so he can bake us some bread. We have fat drippings left, and we can trade beans with Clotilde for some of her goose eggs. Tomorrow, after dark, when the curfew is on, we go."

Gavin nodded. "Fa always said you had a quick wit, sister." He knelt to lay a fire on the flat stone in the middle of the floor.

The smoke rose in gray threads through the hole in the center of the thatched roof. Pearl set a pot of soup on the coals, then she took a cloth and wrapped up the fat they would carry with them.

Gavin opened the chest where they kept their few belongings. "You can wear my shirt and tunic, and my leggings. I'm already too big for them. The new ones you made for Fa will nearly fit me."

He eyed her closely. "We must cut off your hair. Let Sir Geoffrey look for a girl and a boy. We'll be far away, looking like brothers!"

They sat together near the fire, dipping their bread into the soup on the floor between them. When they were done, they set a new rush into the dish and shelled beans until curfew. These they would take with them. The pods they kept to throw in the ox's trough.

Later, Pearl lay wakeful on her straw pallet. If she reached out, she could touch her father, but this did not frighten her. *Fa,* she told him silently, *you've been good to us, and now you even protect us in death. No one will take us away while they think you still live!*

They left at first light, Gavin for the manor fields, Pearl for the baker's with her sack of flour. Faxon's boy was just making up the fire under the huge oven. Faxon Baker stood at a trestle table shaping the dark dough into loaves.

Pearl gave him her sack and watched anxiously as he measured out the flour.

"This will make three loaves," he said. "Two to take and one to leave in payment."

"Six loaves," Pearl said quickly. "Four to take and two to leave."

The baker waved her away with an impatient hand. "You have wrongly measured." His thick red eyebrows moved up and down as he spoke. "Off with you, now!"

Pearl would not be cheated. Faxon Baker was like Gerrold Miller down the road, who ground the serfs' grain into flour for them. Both kept more in payment than their rightful share. Yet it was the law that serfs could not grind their own grain or bake their own bread.

She fixed her blue eyes steadily on his. "I have given you flour for six loaves of black bread and I mean to have four of them!"

Faxon Baker gaped at her in shocked surprise. "Well," he muttered, grudgingly, "be you here at the nooning and you get four loaves. Be you late and you get none!"

Pearl nodded, satisfied, and hurried to her field. Clotilde crouched on the other side of the pathway.

"How goes your Fa?" she asked. Her smile revealed a ragged row of teeth.

"He's worsened. I'll not come a-picking tomorrow."

Clotilde gave a grunt of understanding.

At midday, Pearl closed her sack and swung it over her shoulder. "I'm off to Faxon Baker's for bread. And we need eggs. Will you take some beans for four of your good goose eggs, Clotilde?"

"Aye," said Clotilde, without looking up. "Just help yourself to four of the biggest."

Faxon Baker was standing in his doorway picking his teeth when Pearl arrived. He grunted a greeting and waved toward the four small loaves on the table. Pearl scooped them quickly into her sack before he might change his mind. She walked with measured steps to the turn of the road. Once out of sight of the baker, she ran.

When she came in sight of her own house, she halted. Her breath caught in her throat. Her heart nearly stopped.

Father Alwyn stood at the door, waiting.

THREE

ESCAPE

"GOOD DAY to you, Father." Pearl hoped her voice did not betray her fear. "You have come to see Fa?"

His reply was unexpected. "It's you I've come to see. I thought to find you here with your father."

"I've been to get bread." She swung her sack down between them. She frowned up at him, wondering what she would do if he asked to go inside the house.

But he only reached into his cloak and drew out a string of dried figs. "Sir Geoffrey has returned from a journey and has made me a gift of these. I want to share them with you."

Pearl had never tasted figs. She stared at them until he pushed them into her hand and closed her fingers over them. Tears of relief and gratitude filled her eyes. She knelt at his feet.

"No need to weep," he said softly, raising her up. "Go, now, and tend to your duties."

Pearl watched from the roadside until he had gone. With heavy heart she turned to push the rough door open onto darkness and death. Like all the other huts in the village, hers was windowless. Only a small patch of daylight dropped through the fire hole in the roof.

Pearl needed no other light for her tasks. She took the loaves from her sack and set them on the chest. She poured out some of the beans, swung the sack over her shoulder, and hurried past her father's bed to the door.

A few minutes later, she reached Clotilde's house. Outside, Clotilde's geese waddled up and down in fair imitation of their mistress. Pearl smiled at the thought. On a bench inside the door she found the egg basket. She examined each egg, mindful that Clotilde had said to take four of the biggest.

She emptied her beans into Clotilde's boiling pot. Then she took some straw from a box under the bench and carefully wrapped each egg before putting it in the sack.

Home again, in the dim silence, Pearl laid the fire for supper and set the eggs to boil. The flames' glow danced off the onion bulbs dangling by their dried stems from the roof beam. She pulled the onions down, cut off their stems, and put them on the chest with the bread.

There was the last of the soup to heat, and bread to divide for supper. Pearl looked at the drippings she had wrapped the night before. Who could say when they would safely eat a proper meal again? She hesitated, then cut a generous lump of fat to place on each piece of bread.

The sound of footsteps startled her. Terrified, she watched the door swing open.

"Gavin! You're early!"

"Nay, I'm late." He held the door wide to the setting sun.

Pearl drew him inside. "The day has sped faster than I knew. Oh, Gavin! 'Tis good to have you home!"

"Ah, 'tis good to *be* home!" He squatted near the fire and filled their only bowl from the soup pot.

Pearl took the figs from the chest before he could see them, and held them behind her back. She grinned at him.

He grinned back at her. "What have you there?"

She showed him the string of figs. His look of astonishment made her laugh. "Father Alwyn brought them. A gift to himself from Sir Geoffrey."

His smile faded. "Did he . . . ?"

"Nay, he never asked to come inside the house. He knows nothing. I have let on to no one."

They ate in silence, dipping bread into the bowl of soup between them. When they had finished, Pearl gave them each a fig and put the rest into her pouch.

Gavin took out his knife and cut Pearl's hair. He turned it under like a boy's, just below the ears. Then they changed clothes.

Pearl strode up and down the small room getting accustomed to the feel of the short tunic and the coarse leggings wrapped around her legs. That part was not so difficult. Getting used to the cropped hair would take time. She covered her head with Gavin's close-fitting cap and tied it under her chin.

Gavin laid her dress on the fire. Together they watched it burn. Then Pearl divided the food they would carry, while Gavin stamped out the fire.

Long after the curfew horn had blown they swung their pouches over their shoulders and looped their knife sheaths onto their belts. They stood side by side near their blanket-covered father.

"I think he would know why we leave him, alone and unburied," Gavin said.

Pearl knelt and turned back the blanket. She kissed her father's forehead. "Good-bye, Fa," she whispered.

Suddenly her hand touched something. She cried out and pulled the blanket away.

The dead man's fingers held a cross made of palm.

Pearl gasped. "Father Alwyn!"

Gavin blew out the rushlight. "He must have left that when he brought the figs. Did he want to betray us he would have done so by now, would he not?"

"How can we know? Oh, Gavin, I'm so afraid!"

He answered softly, "So am I."

They closed the door behind them and ran through the dark toward the forest. Not far away a wolf was howling. Closer still, another howled in answer.

FOUR

DISCOVERED

THE GRASS was dark beneath their feet, the sky above them only a shade lighter. Ahead stood the forest, a patch of blackness offering both safety and danger.

Gavin clutched Pearl's shoulder and pulled her down beside him near a clump of gorse bushes. "The moon!" He pointed skyward.

The clouds had parted. Moonlight spilled onto the rusty red of the gorse leaves. It revealed the blurred yellow-white of sheep and the dark hulks of sleeping oxen.

Moments later, another cloud hid the moon. Gavin raced forward. Pearl picked herself up and followed. They reached the fallow fields and joined hands to cross the rough-plowed ridges. They removed their shoes to wade across the pebbly stream and through the swamp on the other side. In the wide-leafed bracken at the forest's edge they paused for breath and knelt to put on their shoes.

"The clouds are breaking up again," Gavin whispered. "Hurry!"

But Pearl had heard something. "Get down!"

They threw themselves flat into the bracken and waited. The swish and crackle of footsteps approached. Pearl's heart beat wildly. Who would be out after curfew? She lay still as death.

The moon was out again. Its light slipped through the leaves. Whoever was coming would see them!

The steps came near. Passed them by. Pearl waited for her heart to stop pounding before she peered out over the leaves. Far away in the moonlight strode a tall figure in a flowing gown. The priest! The only one not bound by curfew.

She jumped at a nearby movement. Gavin grinned at her over the leaves. "Town air is free air!" he said. He led the way on hands and knees into the forest.

It was difficult to keep to a true direction among the trees as they searched for the woodcutter's track. They had to stop often and use their knives to clear a way through tangled vines and underbrush.

When they came to the wide swath cut between winding rows of trees, they halted. Here the earth was rutted from the churning of wagon wheels.

Pearl shivered with fear. "This will take us right past the woodcutter's cottage!"

"Aye," said Gavin. "Pray God he's a sound sleeper!"

They turned onto the rough track. The tall trees rose high above them on either side, leaving a gray ribbon of sky floating overhead. Now and then an owl hooted, or a twig snapped underfoot. The rest was silence. They could hear each other's heavy breathing.

They were nearly abreast of the small hut before they saw it. "The woodcutter's cottage!" Gavin whispered. "Do we go on?"

Pearl peered into the darkness. "The house sits close beside the road. He could waken and hear us. Let's try to get some sleep and watch for him in the morning. We can see which way he takes to go about his work, then go another."

Cautiously they turned back among the trees, looking for a place to rest. Pearl's pouch caught on a branch. She stopped to tug it free and sent a roosting blackbird into flight with a startled squawk. An owl called out in alarm, and a dog barked.

They heard the scraping of a heavy door opening. A flicker of light pricked the darkness as the woodcutter came out of his cottage waving his lantern about.

"Hallo?" he called. "Who comes?"

They stood motionless in the still shadows. Had they come near enough for the dog to find their scent? No, it was running in the opposite direction, barking and thrashing through the underbrush. After what seemed a very long time, the woodcutter whistled. The dog whined in answer, but it left off its search and returned to the hut.

The light disappeared, the door slammed shut. Once more they were left to the silence.

"Now!" said Gavin. They ran for some distance down a path worn smooth by the woodcutter before turning off again among the trees.

Pearl felt the unfamiliar softness of moss beneath her feet. "Oh!" she cried, leaning down to touch the cool moss. "This be a restful place, and far enough from the cottage."

She lay on the moss with her head on her pouch. Gavin flung

himself down beside her. "We'd best waken early, or we'll run into the woodcutter."

But the woodland came awake more quietly than their busy serfs' village. The soft rustling movements of the forest creatures did not disturb their sleep. It was the sharp, triumphant bark of a dog that awakened them.

Gavin grabbed his pouch and knife as he sprang to his feet. Growling, the dog closed in. He was waist high to Gavin. His large head with its short snout and drooping ears was set on a thick neck and powerful shoulders. His coat was the gray-brown of dry earth.

Pearl screamed for Gavin to stand back. She fumbled in her pouch for bread to throw to the beast. The dog barked again and moved toward her. Over the noise of her screams came the call of a man's voice.

"Ho, there, Chop! Have you found them, then?"

Beyond the dog Pearl saw the woodcutter striding toward them.

FIVE

THE WOODCUTTER

"**S**O, YOU HAVE COME!" the woodcutter said. "Steady, Chop, old fellow. Steady!" He paused to take their measure. "You be the runaways, of course. The childer whose Fa is gone, rest his soul."

Pearl and Gavin exchanged terrified glances. How could he know about them so soon? Had they slept for more than one night on their mossy bed?

The woodcutter saw their alarm and smiled. He had gaps in his mouth where teeth had been, though he was still a youngish man. In spite of their fright, the children sensed that his smile was friendly.

"Somebody guessed you were about to run off. Said you'd likely come the forest way. Came to me yester eve and asked could I help you." He rubbed the dog's ears. "Now, when something set the birds a-squawking last night, I says to Chop, 'Ho, 'tis them!' So when he missed your trail at first, I sent him off again this morning to sniff you out."

"But, who . . . ?" Gavin's voice was scratchy with relief. Pearl stood with her hands pressed to her face, staring in disbelief.

"Come," the woodcutter said. "You must be hungry after your night's adventure."

The cottage door was open. Inside, a meal was set out on a trestle table: black bread, cold boiled mutton, boiled beans, and a tankard of cider.

As Pearl stepped inside she noticed something else. Near the pewter tankard lay a string of figs. Father Alwyn! Gavin came through the doorway talking to Chop. He stopped and fell silent. He had seen them, too.

"Let be. Never speak of it," the woodcutter warned. He waved them to the bench. "I'm told you are Gavin and Pearl. Wat's my name. Welcome! Now, eat hearty!"

He rolled a barrel over to the table and sat down, spearing a slab of meat with his knife. He slapped the meat onto a thick piece of bread. He dipped his spoon into the bean pot, tasted, and nodded to his guests.

They wiped their own knives clean on the hems of their tunics and began to eat hungrily.

"Today we cut firewood," Wat told them. "Tomorrow the same. Then we'll take a wagonload to Wallbrooke Town, where my sister lives. Gwen is a weaver, and a widow these ten years. She can keep you hid till she finds proper road company for you. Market days be coming up, and she'll have friends among the folk who come to buy or sell."

"No need to trouble her," Gavin said with a show of confidence. "Only set us on a road that goes somewhere."

Wat washed down his food with a swallow from the tankard.

"Little you know of the world! Even the boldest knight travels only with armed companions."

He wiped his mouth on his sleeve. "Between the towns, in woods and wastelands, lurk wild wolves and wilder men— thieves and murderers, and every kind of outlaw. Only in numbers be there safety, and that none too certain."

He put some of the food into his pouch and the rest in a chest by the wall. "You can trust all to Gwen Weaver. She has an eye for honest folk. She'll see you safely on your way!" He whistled to Chop, who was under the table gnawing on a bone. They followed him outside.

Wat pointed to a bell hanging between two trees. "Whoever comes in search of you will summon me with the bell. They'll not venture further into the forest without me as guide."

He led the way to a shed behind the cottage, where an ox made snuffling noises in its empty feed trough. Wat filled the trough with fodder. "This old fellow's name is Barden," he told them. "Now, let's get to work."

He brought them to a clearing in the woods where a score or more of trees had been felled. These were lying on their sides, already trimmed of branches, waiting for the ax to cut them into hearth-sized logs. A half-loaded wagon stood nearby.

They set to work. Gavin helped Wat with the chopping. Pearl separated the branches. She broke them into kindling sticks and bound them into bundles with vine.

"Might not some traveler come upon us unawares?" she asked Wat. "We would hear no footsteps over the noise we make."

Wat shook his head. "The travelers' road swings wide of the forest. No one comes in here but Sir Geoffrey's man, and he only once a fortnight, to collect my wood money. Father Alwyn stops by now and again to pass the time. And once a year Sir Geoffrey comes himself, to say whereabouts the year's cutting of wood shall be. With him come a few stout serfs who fell the trees."

When Wat finally left his ax in a log and reached for his pouch, they knew it was time for the midday meal. They had scarcely finished when the clanging of the bell startled them. Pearl stared at Wat, numb with fright.

"Off with you, that way!" he said, pointing. "Hide! And make no sound till Chop and I return."

They ran. They found a tangle of vines and bushes and clawed their way through to its center.

"We'll be discovered, do we stay here!" Gavin said. He got up to run again.

Pearl grabbed the tail of his tunic. "Wait! They'll hear us, do we run. Please, trust it to Wat!"

Gavin stayed. He took out his knife. "Do they come for us I'll not be taken."

Long, long moments passed as they crouched there, cramped and sore. A twig snapped and Pearl froze. She pulled her own knife free.

At last they heard Wat's cheerful whistle and Chop's now familiar bark. All was well! They sheathed their knives and hugged each other. Clasping hands, they ran back to the clearing.

"You've naught to fear in the forest now," Wat said as they joined him. "Sir Geoffrey's men have set me to watch for you!"

That night, in the straw near the hearth where embers still hissed and glowed, Pearl lay restless and wakeful. She missed her father and grieved for her loss. She could hear the heavy breathing of Wat and Gavin as they slept. Chop twitched and made small sleep sounds.

She felt so alone! Tears came. She sniffled. The unfamiliar sound woke Chop. He snorted, shook his huge head, and blinked. Seeing her awake also, he pulled himself up and went to her. She buried her face in his fur and wept.

On the third morning, at breakfast, Wat said, "Today we finish with the loading and leave for Wallbrooke." He gave them some mutton and small turnips for their pouches.

Pearl lingered in the doorway, looking back into the little room that had been home for such a short while. With a sigh, she turned away. She found that Wat was watching.

"You'll have better than this one day," he said.

She laughed in disbelief. What could be better than a home, a hearth, good food—and nothing to fear?

Gavin had brought Barden around. Now they all stepped briskly to the clearing. Wat hitched Barden to the front of the wagon. Then, while Pearl and Gavin tied up the last of the kindling, he fashioned a hollow among the logs and bundles on the back of the wagon.

"Best you ride in there," he said, pointing to the hollow.

Pearl crawled inside, then Gavin. Wat rearranged the kindling around them. Presently they heard the wagon creak and felt it sag as Wat climbed onto the driver's seat.

"Ho, Barden!" he shouted. The ox pulled. The wheels turned slowly and the wagon moved out of the clearing and onto the track. Chop ran back and forth, before and behind, flushing small forest creatures from the underbrush in his excitement.

Inside the wagon, Pearl was thrown against Gavin. He reached for her hand and squeezed it. *Freedom!* his tightening grip seemed to say. *Freedom!* her fingers answered.

Up ahead, Wat began to whistle.

SIX

MATILL MAKEJOYE

FOR SOME TIME the wagon lurched and rolled along the track. When Pearl finally felt the sun's warmth through the kindling, her heart leaped. They were out of the forest and on the open road!

"We're coming to the bridge at the river crossing," Wat said at last. "I must pass the time of day with Diccon Tollman, else he'll think something's amiss." He began to whistle again.

The wagon jerked to a stop. "Ho, there, Diccon!" Wat called. "How goes it this fine day?"

"Well enough," Diccon replied. "Plenty of honest farthings, with folk crossing over for market days. To judge by your load, you be fresh from the greenwood."

"That I be." Wat cleared his throat. "And this be payment for my ox, wagon, load, and my own self." Coins jingled as they changed hands.

"What? No Chop with you this day? Ho, he has swum across! Well, he still pays his toll."

Wat laughed. "Does he now? And will you catch him for it? Well, here, then, and good day to you."

"Look sharp as you go," Diccon Tollman said. "One of Sir Geoffrey's serfs has passed on, God rest him, and his two childer have run off, they say."

"Oh, they have? And Sir Geoffrey has sent out to get them back, I don't doubt."

"He has, and with a reward for their finding. But with little luck, as it happens. The earth might have opened up and swallowed them, for the signs they left. Poor babes! They'll end their days with a sly beggar who'll teach them how to be cutpurses by day and beat them by night for not stealing enough."

"Well, we can hope that they learn quickly how to get along in this sad and evil world."

"Best to hope they get caught! Sir Geoffrey be not near so cruel a master as some, from the tales I hear in this very tollhouse."

"Right you be, Diccon, my friend," Wat said, as the wagon began to move on. "And you can be sure, do I see them, I'll tell them you said so!"

"Good morrow to you, then," Diccon called after him. "And to your sister, Gwen Weaver."

The wagon clattered over the stone bridge. All Pearl's fears had returned with the tollman's words. Where would she and Gavin go? Among what sort of folk? She thought of the sly beggar who would make them steal, and her flesh rose up in bumps.

They left the bridge. The familiar feel of the road returned.

Pearl heard Chop shake the water from his fur as he caught up with them.

"Ahead lies the town," Wat said. "We'll pass through the gate and ride down Market Street. No doubt the gatekeeper is warned about you, so be still as can be."

The town noises met them: wooden wheels on the cobbled street, drivers shouting one another out of the way, street sellers calling their wares, children shrieking high above the yowling of dogs. A man's gruff voice sounded over the din. Wat drew Barden to a halt.

"Ho, there, Wat Woodman! I've been waiting for you. Have you heard about the runaways? I'm to inspect all carts and wagons—but only a beetle could hide in that load of wood. What say you?"

"Only a beetle," Wat replied, laughing.

The wagon moved forward again. As it struck the cobblestones, some of the kindling shifted. A bundle broke loose and slid down, threatening to reveal their hiding place. Pearl and Gavin reached up to hold it.

Suddenly the wagon turned sharply. The sounds grew dim. They seemed to be in a quiet lane. As they halted again, Pearl heard the swing and thump of a weaver's loom.

The loom twanged and thwacked once more, and was still. A light, pleasant voice called Wat's name. Quick, short steps hurried toward them. Then Wat was at the back of the wagon pulling the kindling out of the way.

"Look sharp about you, Gwen. Be we alone?"

"Aye, there's no one about."

"Then see what I bring you! Runaways, poor childer. Into the house with them whilst I unyoke old Barden."

Pearl and Gavin crawled out to find Gwen smiling them a welcome. She was small, not much taller than Pearl, and older than Wat. A clean white cap covered all but a few wisps of her gray-brown hair. Her dress of scarlet wool was nearly hidden by the white apron that reached to the tops of her scarlet felt shoes.

As Gwen looked more closely at Pearl, her blue eyes filled with sudden warmth. "Why, Wat, this be a young girl in boy's garb! Oh, come in, come in! You must be a-frighted near to death." She drew Pearl toward the open door, beckoning Gavin to follow.

This house was far grander than the huts of the serfs' village. It was two stories high, of dark wood and bright yellow plaster. Its thatched roof was peaked and deep-sloping. There were two small windows downstairs, their shutters thrown back to let the light fall on Gwen's loom. A steep outside stairway led to the floor above.

They stepped inside onto clean, fresh-smelling rushes. Rolls of woven cloth were laid out on a trestle board along the far wall. There was some green stuff on the loom.

Gwen led the way to a room behind the workroom; this was her kitchen and living place. She set about fixing a meal. Pearl and Gavin loosened their pouches and laid them on the table.

"We've food to share," Pearl offered shyly. "Beans and bread, and a bit of fat. Even some boiled eggs!"

"The bread and eggs, right enough," Gwen agreed. "They want to spoil, and I can give you fresh of both when you leave. But keep the rest."

She looked at Pearl again. "We be nearly of a height, and small-built. I'll give you a dress to wear when you go, and a cloak." She clacked her tongue and frowned. "There's naught we can do about that shorn hair. But with so much of the fever about, folk will think it fell out with the sickness."

Wat came in and they sat down two by two on benches alongside the table. Gwen put a wooden trencher of food between each pair. Pearl and Gavin grinned at each other over the generous portions of salt herring, black bread, and hot cabbage boiled with drippings.

"Now," Gwen said, "tomorrow Wat and I go to market. We'll find a likely band of travelers who will let you join them, do you promise to work for your keep and give them no trouble."

That night Pearl slept on a mat in the kitchen with Gwen. Wat and Gavin made straw beds for themselves upstairs.

In the morning, Wat wrapped Gwen's rolls of cloth in oilskin and tied them onto the side of the wagon. Gwen came out as he was putting Barden to the yoke. They left with a final word of caution for Pearl and Gavin to stay inside, out of sight.

Shortly after midday, Gwen returned with a young woman. She was about twenty years old, and tall, with bright brown eyes. Her long black hair was gathered into a net of green linen. Her dress was a merry shade of green, though it was worn and frayed at the hem and at the edges of the long sleeves. A green purse hung from a belt of braided blue wool. Strapped to the woman's back was a boar-skin bag of odd shape.

She introduced herself with a friendly smile. "I am Matill. Matill Makejoye I call myself, because making joy with my good friend here is my trade." Matill opened her bag and showed them its contents.

Pearl gasped with delight. A guitar!

"You're a minstrel!" Gavin said with awe in his voice. "The same as come sometimes to play at the manor house for Sir Geoffrey on feast days."

"Nay," Matill answered with a wry grin, "only a poor road minstrel singing for farthings or for a basket of turnips. Not like those who live grandly amongst the lords and the ladies!"

Pearl's gaze had lingered on Matill's gaudy garb. Worn and faded it was, yet she had never seen anything so splendid. "I think you be grand enough for any gentle," she murmured.

"Well said!" Matill came forward and threw her arms around Pearl. She released her just as suddenly, laughing at Pearl's look of astonishment. She took her hands and turned them palms up.

"What fine, long fingers. Nimble, too, I think. The hands of a musician! Would you like to be a minstrel your own self?"

Pearl's eyes widened. She nodded, speechless.

"And you?" Matill turned to Gavin. "What can you do?"

"N-n-nothing! Plow a furrow. Winnow grain," Gavin stammered, his hands outspread.

Matill's bright laugh filled the room. In the space of an eye's wink she had snatched a round cheese from the table and tossed it.

"Catch!" she cried, and in that instant when his hands reached out for it she tossed him another.

"So!" she said when he had caught them both. "'Tis a juggler you be!" She gave Gwen a nod of satisfaction.

"They'll do. You did well to bring me here. These two can fill the gaps made by those tumblers who left us last year. The girl looks sharp and the lad has his wits about him. A pity about that hair, but 'twill grow out in time."

Matill spoke gently to Pearl. "Will you come along with us, then? No one will beat you, I promise. But you'll work hard, and you'll share every coin or cabbage you earn, as do we all. We are five in our troupe: Widsith Gleeman, my brother and a minstrel like myself. Joan Lightfoot, the most graceful of dancers. Will Scarface, the finest juggler in all of England. And Rob the miller, who walks tightropes with Garth, his monkey."

"Oh, we'll come, and gladly!" Pearl answered, marveling at their good fortune. Gavin made no reply.

But it was settled. They would go with Matill Makejoye on the day after next.

SEVEN

THE PILGRIM

IT WAS early morning. Pearl and Gavin sat at their last meal with Gwen and Wat. Pearl forced the thick porridge down. She had already become fond of Gwen and Wat and hated to leave this pleasant home. Tears splashed down her face and onto the table.

Gwen saw them. She leaned across and touched Pearl's hand. "You be so like the child I lost, long ago. It grieves me that you must leave us!"

Pearl dried her eyes with her fists. She rubbed her hands down the blue dress Gwen had given her.

"Now, then," said Gwen with forced cheerfulness, getting up from the bench, "you must take some of this good salt herring with you." She wrapped some for Pearl's pouch.

Wat drained his mug and strode to the door. "The sun's coming up. Best we be off before the whole town wakens."

They followed him outside. Tearfully, Gwen and Pearl embraced. Gavin made an awkward bow and added his thanks to Pearl's. Then they climbed into the wagon and crawled under the blanket Gwen had put there.

On Market Street the town's visiting buyers and sellers were already preparing to leave. Pearl could hear the clink of harness, the scrape of boxes and barrels being loaded onto carts and wagons. Here and there a shouted command or call of farewell rose above the low drone of voices.

"Now!" Wat commanded. Pearl and Gavin threw off the blanket and slid to the ground. Pearl was clutched by the arm and rushed forward toward a blue wagon hitched to a mule and loaded with wooden chests and leather pouches.

"Quickly! Up!" Matill gave her a boost and jumped up after her. Just as quickly, a tall young man heaved Gavin over the side. Again they were under a cover. They lay there, getting their breath back.

Matill whispered, "You have little to fear, I think. They looked for you all over the marketplace these three days. But last night we talked with the gatekeeper. He says the search is off—hereabouts, at least. Once we get through the gate, you're safe!"

The wagon jerked forward and rolled at a steady pace over the cobblestones. Matill strummed her guitar and sang, joined by another woman who sat nearby. Pearl could just see the pointed toes of her brown leather shoes.

The wagon slowed, stopped briefly to wait its turn through the gate, then moved on. "Safe!" Matill whispered.

They rode for an endless time before the blanket was snatched away. Pearl stared up into Matill's dark eyes.

"Here they be, Joan!" Matill said. "Our two new goslings, Pearl and Gavin."

Joan could not be older than sixteen, Pearl thought. Her eyes were uptilted and of pale blue color. Her brown hair was nearly hidden beneath a rose-colored coverchief that matched her dress. She smiled, revealing an even row of teeth.

"Joan Lightfoot," Matill was saying. "And up at the reins sits Rob Miller with Garth, his monkey."

Rob grinned and raised a hand in greeting. He looked to be in his late twenties. He had thick, straw-colored hair and amber eyes as intent as an owl's. He sat with an easy grace, his slim body moving in rhythm to the bouncing of the wagon. From his shoulder the monkey eyed the newcomers with silent curiosity.

"Rob cannot speak," Matill explained. "He was a miller, once, to a cruel lord. One day he spoke his mind and for punishment lost his tongue. Well, neither can his monkey speak, yet they make a clever pair."

Pearl caught Gavin's bleak stare. What would happen to *them* if they were caught?

From behind they heard a deep voice. "Mind your manners, Matill. Or have you forgotten all about us?"

For the first time Pearl noticed two men walking along the road behind the wagon. Matill wrinkled her nose and wagged her head toward the taller one. "My young and sometimes foolish brother, Widsith Gleeman."

"Matill jokes," Joan said in a chiding voice. "Widsith likes to tease, but he has a wise head on his shoulders."

Widsith was dark, like his sister, and two or three years younger. He walked with big strides, swinging his arms in time with his steps. His grin was wide and his eyes held mischief as he waved to Pearl and Gavin.

"The quiet fellow there is our dear Will Scarface," Matill continued. "He'll teach Gavin the art of juggling. His father was a blacksmith, and so should Will have been, but for a traveling band of players who came through town when he was a boy. On the morning they left, Will left with them."

Will must have been Widsith's age. His fiery red hair framed a wide, round face pocked with scars from some long-ago illness. He was short and husky, wide at the shoulders and thick-waisted. He took two steps to Widsith's one, and to Pearl he did not look agile enough to be a juggler—not until he plucked some rings from his belt, tossed them high in the air, and caught them neatly as he bowed to those in the wagon. Pearl gaped and marveled at his deftness.

Joan laid her hand gently over Pearl's. "I was orphaned, as you are, when I was young," she said. "I was but six years old, and went to my grandmother. She taught me all about herbs and healing, and I loved her. She died when I was fourteen."

"How came you to be a dancer?" Gavin asked.

"My uncle was a street musician in London. He took me when my grandmother died, and I learned to dance to his bagpipes. We were playing at Smithfield, just outside the walls of London, when we met Matill and Widsith. They were getting up a troupe of performers to play the fairs and market days in the towns all around."

"Our own mother we never knew," Matill said. "But our father was a wandering minstrel who took us with him. As soon as we could hold a guitar and blow on a flute, he taught us how to play."

She clasped her hands around her knee and continued, "Our father is old now. His hands are crippled with age and he no longer plays his music. Widsith and I carry on his work, playing the towns from late spring till early autumn. Then we all winter in London in his house on Kitchen Lane."

Pearl had been watching Matill and Joan with admiration and envy. "Minstrels come to the manor house on feast days," she said shyly. "All the serfs go to the celebration. But never have I seen a—a female minstrel among them."

Matill laughed. "Most females be hearth-bound with husband and childer and enormous responsibilities. Yet we are not all cut from the same cloth. Certainly not I!"

"Nor I," said Joan, "though I look forward to the time when I'll have a husband. I'll choose a trouper like myself."

Matill jabbed Pearl in the ribs with her elbow and winked at Gavin. "She means a trouper like my brother!"

Joan blushed. Plainly, this teasing was not to her liking.

Soon Rob brought the mule to a halt beneath a great twisted tree at the side of the road. A glance at the sky told Pearl it was time for the midday meal.

She helped Joan spread a blanket under the tree. Matill handed Gavin and Will a cheese and some loaves of bread from one of the chests. Rob took out leather flasks of cider. Widsith unhitched the mule, whom he called Mule, to let him graze. He stroked the beast's face with obvious affection and was rewarded with a soft, nuzzling kiss.

After they had eaten, Gavin led Mule into the wood, where, Widsith said, a small brook ran. The others rested on the blanket or in the grass.

Suddenly Widsith sat up. Gavin had reappeared, holding on to something slung across Mule's back. "Ho! See what Gavin

brings us! Someone wearing pilgrim's garb." He sprang to his feet and ran to help Gavin.

They lowered the stranger onto the blanket. The man's long gray hair was damp and matted. His face was the color of candle wax, and lined with wrinkles. Will held a flask to his lips.

"Ar! Ar!" the man moaned, choking on gulps of cider. He tried to sit up, thrashing his arms wildly.

"Poor fellow, he wanders in his head," Joan said. "Let me see does he have a fever."

Gavin came forward with a large oilskin bag. "He'll want this near him. I had to pry it loose of his fingers when I lifted him." He put the bag on the blanket and laid the man's blue-veined hand on top of it. At once the stranger ceased his struggles and lay still, gasping for breath.

Widsith was right—the sick man wore pilgrim's garb. Pearl had seen pilgrims come through the village. They were pious souls who wandered the world from one holy shrine to another. This man wore the pilgrim's brown robe. Pinned to his wide-brimmed hat, which Gavin had also rescued, were a number of small lead badges that represented the different shrines he had visited. A tiny glass bottle of holy water hung from a cord around his neck.

Joan dipped a cloth into some cider and sprinkled it with dried herbs from her herb box. Then she folded the cloth, wound it around the man's head and neck, and tied it securely. Then she fixed a hot, spiced brew and made him drink.

"Ar, ar," he repeated softly. Then he was asleep.

They made a sling of the blanket and gently lifted him into the wagon. Joan climbed up beside him, calling to Pearl to join her.

It was Will's turn at the reins. The others all trailed on foot.
"Will he die?" Pearl asked anxiously, thinking of her father.

Joan shrugged. "He has a high fever. My herb potions be
strong, but if he's been ill for long . . ."

Pearl sat on a chest near the pilgrim, staring at the oilskin
bag. Whatever it held must be precious to him, that he should
cry out for it in his delirium.

Late in the afternoon, Will turned the wagon onto a meadow.
Widsith dug a hole for their roasting fire while Gavin and Pearl
hunted stones for lining it. Matill brought out two plucked fowls
rolled up in wet cloth.

They wrapped onions and pieces of meat together in leaves
and placed them in the fire pit. Around these they arranged
the turnips Wat had given Pearl. They topped the whole with
clods of earth and waited for their meal to cook.

Matill took up her guitar and sang.

> "Oh, whither and whither I wander, I wander!
> Over the field and into the hollow
> Come follow, come follow!
> Where birds are singing and sheep bells ringing,
> And lambkins over the grass are springing!
>
> "And listen! Now, listen! Oh, listen to me!
> Sinner and saint should wander free
> Year after year with never a fear
> Till the sun has set on the king's highway."

"Ar! Ar!" It was the pilgrim again, thrashing about in the

wagon. Joan hurried to give him something to drink from the small flask she had looped to her belt.

"His head feels some cooler to the touch. I think the headcloth be driving out the fever."

Widsith chortled. " 'Tis not the headcloth but the brew you give him! That would drive the devil out!"

They all gathered at the wagon as Joan helped the sick man sit up against her knee. The wildness had left his eyes. His face had taken on some color.

He looked anxiously around until he saw the bag. With trembling fingers he reached for it. Pearl pushed it toward him. Carefully he drew out a boat-shaped thing of dark shiny wood. From keel to high curved prow were strung thirteen strings of brightly colored silk, each ending in a tassel along the neck of the prow.

Matill gasped. "A harp! And such an odd one. That's what he was trying to say! He wanted to make sure we had his harp safe. Such a beautiful thing, no wonder."

"Never have I seen its like," said Widsith. "Have you strength to speak, pilgrim? What do they call you? You be amongst friends, so have no fear."

The pilgrim looked from one to another. "Friends you be, and that I know, for you have plucked me straight from the edge of the grave. Tom of Margate thanks you."

He lay back against Joan's knee.

"Our warm meal is about done," Will said. "Once you have tucked some of that into your gullet, your strength will return."

"Aye," said Joan, "and for the while it takes to make you whole again, we'll all watch out for you."

EIGHT

PEARL IN THE EGG

THEY WERE on their way again at sunrise. Will Scar-face took some wooden rings from the wagon. "Walk with me as we go," he said to Gavin. "We've three long days ahead of us to Greencastle. I'll make you a juggler of sorts before we come onto the place."

"And I'll teach Pearl a song as we ride with Tom Pilgrim," Matill decided.

Thus began three of the happiest days Pearl had ever known. At first she timidly mouthed the words of the song as Matill sang it for her. She was astonished when Matill told her her voice was both sweet and well-pitched.

Matill's frank pleasure gave Pearl confidence. "You sing true and have an ear for music. The rest will come in time."

Gavin did not fare so well. More often than not he missed the rings Will tossed him and had to chase after them. The missing and the chasing put him out of sorts.

"No need to feel unhopeful," Will said encouragingly. " 'Tis all just a matter of training."

Later, as they lay ready for sleep under the night sky, Pearl watched the embers glowing in the fire they had laid to keep the wild beasts away. She felt happy and safe.

"Is this new life of ours not Godsent?" she whispered to Gavin. When he made no reply, she nudged him with her toe. "Be you asleep so soon, brother?"

"Not asleep," he said at last. "Thinking."

"Of what? Of how you will one day be the juggler Will is?" She smiled into the darkness.

"Thinking that the wanderer's life is not for me. I dream of living in a fine town house, doing important work."

"Making folk happy is important work."

"Of course. But tossing rings and rolling hoops and playing the fool is not my way."

Presently she heard him snort in sleep. But she lay awake long after, staring up at the stars. Surely Gavin had been only air-building! Now that they had found this safe new life, he would not throw it all away.

"Do that, my brother, and you play the fool in earnest!" she said softly.

Tom Pilgrim's strength was returning. When he could sit up, he let Pearl hold the harp. He told her how he had come by it.

" 'Tis from Burma, a magical land, I am told. See this fine sounding board? 'Tis made from the hide of the buffalo, a fantastic water beast. In the Holy Land I nursed a dying old Crusader who had this harp from a sailor who had it from a Turk. God alone knows how the Turk came onto it."

He explained about the Crusades. Off and on, for nearly two hundred years, Christian knights had been waging war against the Turks who had captured Jerusalem. "Our knights fight bravely and hard," Tom said sadly, "yet the Holy City remains in the hands of the invaders."

As Pearl listened, she held the curved neck of the harp over her arm and stroked the beautiful dark wood.

"You sweep the strings, so, with the flat of your fingers," Tom said. "To change the tune you push the strings up or down the neck, like this."

Pearl ran her fingers over the strings. She warmed with pleasure as the sweet music followed her movement.

"This harp needs a minstrel's voice," Tom said. "It is meant to accompany song. Sing what you have just learned, Pearl. See if you can play as I showed you."

Pearl tried the strings a few times, and sang:

"Over the hills and into the hollow
   Where sheep bells ring, come follow, come follow!
   Though the sun be fierce or the wind be strong,
   Come hither, come hither, and follow my song,
   Which beckons and beckons, now low, now loud,
   As the white dust blows in a swirling cloud."

Her strumming was sometimes off-key, and not always in time with her song. No matter. They applauded her anyway.

"You're a minstrel born!" Matill exclaimed. "I knew it by

those fine, long fingers. One day we'll find you a harp of your own, Pearl."

Pearl smiled her delight. Of course no other harp could be as perfect as this. She loved it! But this was Tom's. Some other would have to do for her. She looked up to find him watching her and felt her face flush. Had he seen into her thoughts?

He had! His look was tender as he said, "It seems to have been made just for you. Surely no voice has ever suited it so well."

The fair was on when they reached Greencastle. The mingled odors of burning charcoal, roasting meat, and animal dung told them where the fairground was.

They joined the noisy groups of people making their slow way along the street. Pearl glanced back over the bobbing heads at Gavin, who trailed far behind. His mouth hung open. His head turned in every direction so as not to miss the wonders he was seeing for the first time.

So I must look my own self, Pearl thought. She had never seen a town. She knew only the sound and smell of Wallbrooke, and the little she had been able to see from Gwen's house.

Yet Greencastle was but a niggling place, so Tom said. "Naught but a bug's splat on the great map of England. Nothing like to the size of London, or even of Bristol."

The fairground was at the other edge of town. Pearl caught her breath as they rode out through the gate. Half the world must be here among the tents and booths, buying and selling with many a loud bargain between, and everyone talking at once.

Widsith brought Mule to a halt in the meadow behind a row

of booths. Matill spread out a blanket for Tom. Pearl and Joan had helped him from the cart and were seating him when the others caught up with them.

They set to work at once. Will pulled down the sides of the wagon and gave them to Gavin, who propped them up against a tree. Widsith tethered Mule in the grass and returned to the wagon to move their chests and pouches under it. Rob began setting up the poles for his tightropes.

Joan and Pearl took a bucket to fetch water for Mule. They returned to the sound of Widsith piping a shrill note on his flute. He stood in the center of the wagon, which was now converted into a stage, trying to get attention.

"Come and spend a pleasant hour with us!" he shouted. "Here you see Widsith Gleeman, my own self." He played a tune on his flute to a sprinkling of applause.

"Matill Makejoye and her singing guitar," Widsith announced. Matill leaped up beside him and played a rousing song. The applause grew.

"Joan Lightfoot, queen of dance!" Joan whirled around the stage on her toes, slim and graceful. She stopped on the other side of Widsith. More people had gathered, and the applause grew louder.

"Now," said Widsith, warming to his task, "I give you Will Scarface and Gavin, his apprentice. Count the rings they juggle betwixt them! Their nimble fingers will play tricks on you, however quick your eye."

Will and Gavin jumped onto the wagon, tossing their rings and catching them. Pearl held her breath. Gavin was trying hard not to make a mistake. He dropped a ring! He caught it on his

foot and tossed it high. Everyone laughed, thinking this was part of the show.

When it was over, Gavin's face was the same flaming red as Will's hair. He glowered and jerked away when Will clapped him on the shoulder and said, "Well enough done!"

Widsith piped for attention again. "Rob Miller and Garth, his monkey!"

Rob gave Garth a short staff and placed him on a low rope stretched between two short poles. The monkey spread out his arms, holding the staff in front of him. He balanced himself carefully on the rope and began to walk. Rob climbed to the higher rope. Will handed him up his staff.

Widsith played while the two made their way to the ends of their ropes and back again. The crowd thrilled to their skill and daring. Pearl, sitting with Tom, was lost in the pleasure of watching when Widsith called out her name.

"And now, good friends, I give you Pearl, our youngest minstrel, with her magical harp from Burma!"

Pearl was stunned. Tom thrust the harp into her hands and prodded her forward. Matill pulled her up onto the wagon.

"Sing!" Matill hissed in her ear. "You've naught to fear. See, I will join you." She pushed Pearl down onto the chest Widsith had left onstage for a stool.

Pearl's head pounded. Her fingers trembled as she balanced the harp on her knee. She glanced reproachfully up at Widsith, whose merry grin made her smile in spite of her discomfort.

Matill strummed her guitar and began the song. Pearl took it up in a wavering voice. Then she gained courage, singing as she played. Though she thrilled to the applause that greeted her efforts, she was glad when the song was done.

For an hour or more the troupe jollied the crowds. Each time Widsith and Gavin took the straw baskets out among them, even the most niggardly dropped in a farthing. It was not often they were entertained by female minstrels. This was worth a farthing!

By the next day, word of their first performance had spread, and the troupe played to an expectant audience. Gavin dropped a ring again. This time it rolled away. The monkey caught it and tossed it back.

Seeing that this had pleased the folk, Gavin tossed him another. Garth ran off with it, to the delight of all but Gavin.

It was Pearl's turn. Matill answered the plea in her eyes and accompanied her again. In the middle of the song she stopped and stepped back, leaving Pearl to go on alone.

After a moment's alarm, Pearl plunged on.

> "Listen! Oh, listen! Oh, listen to me!
> Sinner and saint should wander free
> Year after year with never a fear
> Till the sun has set on the king's highway."

Pearl soon became aware of the crowd's good-humored support, even when she suddenly forgot her lines. She hesitated briefly, then made up new lines of her own.

> "For the world is fair and the world is wide . . .
> Let peasant and prince step along with pride.
> Let the broad highway be an open way
> Where whither and whither I wander, I wander.

"Then follow, come follow!
Over the hills and into the hollow!
If the way be short or the way be long
Come follow, oh, follow, come follow my song."

It was over! The crowd clapped and stamped and clamored for more. Matill pulled Pearl to her feet. "Well done!" she said. "But what was that 'peasant and prince' all about?"

Pearl giggled. "I made that up. I forgot the words." Matill's surprised stare delighted her.

Later, around their fire, Matill said, "Pearl will be a true minstrel one day—a maker of songs, even! For all her life the music has been locked up inside her, till now. She needed only a prod in the right place to send it spilling out, like—like the stuff of an egg when the shell is tapped."

Widsith snapped his fingers. "That gives us her name, Matill! We'll call her Pearl in the Egg! What better name for a minstrel?"

Rob clapped his approval. His amber eyes gave Pearl the praise his poor tongue could not. They smiled at each other over Garth's head as the monkey screeched and clapped also.

"What do we call Gavin?" Joan asked.

Will grinned at Gavin. "Well, young apprentice, what say you to that?"

Gavin did not return the smile. "I want no name till I be free. Then I'll call myself Gavin Freeman!"

"Free!" Widsith said. "So long as you are with us you be free. We travel where we will, with no one to say us nay."

Gavin waved toward Pearl. "We are serfs still. Sir Geoffrey can take us back, does he find us."

Will laughed. "Look at Rob. He was born a serf, just as you. He ran away. And he has outlived his master!"

Pearl looked pleadingly at her brother. "Gavin yearns for the town life," she explained. "But he is only air-building. He will change his mind in time."

Even as she spoke, Gavin's eyes gave the lie to her words. She felt her heart turn over.

NINE

DANGER

BETWEEN PERFORMANCES on the last day at Greencastle, Pearl went with Matill and Joan for a final tour of the fairground. They were soon drawn to the sound of music coming from a booth where two tumblers were performing.

After the tumblers came a man playing the bagpipes and a woman who danced. Pearl watched them, wondering if she would ever be so at ease in front of an audience.

Matill poked her and pointed at a small group of young men standing in front of them. They wore elegant white and blue tunics and yellow hose. They carried musical instruments strapped to their backs.

"That's what you must strive for," Matill said. "You must catch the eye of a rich gentle. Become minstrel to some great lord or lady. Aye, that's the life!"

Pearl looked closely at the young minstrels, who were chatting merrily together. "Why not you?" she asked Matill. "Why are you not all in the service of some gentle?"

Matill made a face. "We have yet to catch the eye of a gentle! That's our misfortune. But you are young yet, Pearl. You have time to become one of the finest minstrels in the land, and to draw the attention of some wealthy lord."

"And should you not," Joan added, squeezing Pearl's hand, "you can stay with us. You won't regret it. We do well enough!"

"Aye, well enough," Matill echoed, "though there have been times when all we earned was a shower of rotten eggs, just because we are women a-trouping. Yet there have been times when our purse overflowed for the very same reason!"

Pearl's gaze had moved from the party of musicians to the performers on the stage. Suddenly she stiffened.

Near the end of the booth, one face stood out from among the others. Heavy-lidded eyes, turned-down mouth, broad nose—Jack Bowman!

Pearl turned quickly away, pretending not to have noticed him, fearful of drawing his gaze toward her. He had seen her but once, she reminded herself. Her hair had been waist-long then, her face hot and smudged with the bark of the wood she had gathered. She slipped behind Joan, fighting down her panic. Surely he would not recognize her now!

When she dared to look again, he was strolling back toward the fairground entrance.

"Come," Matill said, "let's buy something for supper."

Pearl hesitated. Should she tell Matill? Matill was already leading the way to another booth. Anxiously Pearl looked around. The bowman was gone. She hurried to catch up with the two women, who were dickering with a man over the price of fried eels.

They settled the matter of the eels, then bought some sugared quinces.

"Oh, look!" Joan said. "Let's visit the gypsy." She pointed across the way to a leather tent painted with strange signs and symbols. Again Pearl followed, looking back over her shoulder, searching for the dreaded face.

An old woman crouched on a mat outside the tent. She took their money with a grimy hand and a sour glare.

Inside, a young woman sat at a small table. She wore a pale blue dress decorated with glass beads. On her dark hair she wore a white lace coverchief.

There were cards on the table, each with two odd markings on it. The gypsy motioned them to the bench opposite her.

"Your name?" she asked Matill. Matill told her. "An odd one, that," said the gypsy, looking puzzled. "Give me the proper spelling of it."

Matill laughed. "Could I but read and write, do you think I'd be sitting here in this stinking tent? Rather I'd be mistress of a fine house, commanding you to come to me!"

The gypsy gave a grunt of impatience. "Then say the name again, slowly."

"Ma–till," Matill said. "I have never been called else, though I was christened Maude at birth."

The gypsy's black eyes flashed. "Maude! Why did you not say so at the start?"

She selected five cards from the others. "Each card bears a letter of your name. Each letter, as you see, has its own number.

I hold the cards in my hands, so, and the numbers vibrate. They tell me what lies in your future."

Matill sat up straighter and waited with interest while the gypsy frowned over the cards.

"You will have your fine house," she said. Matill made little dark arches of her eyebrows.

"You will make a good marriage. You will travel to lands you have only dreamed of."

Matill hooted. "Look!" She pulled at her worn dress. "This will tell you that I am neither a pilgrim nor a gentle, to go a-wandering all over the world. This will tell you the sort of marriage I am like to make!"

The gypsy scowled. "You need not laugh. Do I say it, then it will be so!"

She turned suddenly to Joan and barked, "Your name?" Joan jumped and answered at once. With a slender finger she slid the cards into a row in front of her. She picked them up and held them for a moment.

"Good fortune awaits you. But it will not come without sadness. A lost love, I think. Yet this will pass, and joy will follow."

Joan snickered behind her fingers, though she held her tongue. Beside her, Matill hooted again.

The gypsy chose not to notice. She slapped the cards down and glared at Pearl.

"Pearl!" Pearl answered before she was asked. She looked straight into the dark eyes.

The gypsy slid the cards forward. She sat for a long while, holding them. Pearl fidgeted on the bench. The gypsy frowned and rubbed her forehead.

"Well?" Matill's voice had an edge to it. "We have paid our money. Tell us what the cards say."

The gypsy held the cards against her closed eyelids for a moment. Then she spread them out on the table. "For fair or for foul, I will say it. Your life will be grand beyond belief! One day you will be friend to a king!"

Pearl was too astonished to speak.

"Well, I don't believe *that!*" Matill snapped. She stood up as a signal to the others to leave.

"Nor do I," Joan said, reaching for Pearl's hand, and they marched out.

"Nor would I believe it myself of such a one," the gypsy called after them, "were it not that I make no mistakes. But hear me! I have not told all. The road to a royal palace is fraught with danger. Only by using her wits and a measure of courage will the girl walk it safely!"

As they returned to their camp, Joan and Matill made sport of their fortunes.

Pearl was silent. The gypsy was wrong, of course, about a king. But she was right about one thing. The road Pearl walked was a dangerous one. Jack Bowman had trailed after her all the way to Greencastle!

A sudden thought made her stop where she was. The troupe had one last performance here. Pearl could never face that audience again, knowing the bowman might lurk among them.

"What's the matter?" Joan asked, stopping suddenly. "Pearl, you're pale as death!"

"I feel sick," Pearl said. "Matill, I'll not be able to sing any more today."

TEN

FLIGHT

WHEN THEY reached their camp, Matill pushed Pearl gently down onto the blanket next to Tom, who had been dozing with his back against a tree. The others were at the wagon, drinking cider and watching the fairgoers.

Pearl's thoughts clawed wildly inside her head, like trapped squirrels. What to do? Should she play sick until she learned whether the bowman had actually spotted her? If she and Gavin were discovered, might the whole troupe be punished for taking them in? Would Matill make Pearl and Gavin leave if she knew danger lurked so near? And if they left, where would they go?

Yet Pearl *had* to tell Gavin—she must keep him from taking part in the next performance, ask him what he thought they should do.

Joan was searching through her herb box. "Whereabouts do you feel unwell, love? Stomach? Chest? Be you dizzy?"

She brought out a sprig of mugwort and tied it around Pearl's neck. "This, and some bitters, should cure whatever ails you. I'll fix you some."

"She is so pale," Matill said to Tom. "This came on so suddenly! Feel her hand, how cold it is."

Pearl pulled her hand away and tried to get up. She had to see Gavin. "Please, I'll be all right," she pleaded.

Tom was watching her curiously. "This be no ordinary upset," he said. "The child has had some terrible fright, I think. What has happened, Pearl?"

Pearl sucked in a long, shuddering breath. All three were looking at her now, their eyes filled with questions and concern.

"Please," she said again, turning to Matill, "we are all in terrible danger!"

Matill opened her mouth. Shut it. Gave Pearl a long, level stare. "I'll get the others," she said finally.

"Drink this." Joan handed Pearl a leather mug. "It should help settle you."

Pearl drank the bitter brew. Matill returned with the men, all sober-faced and wondering. Pearl sighed. Joan was right: the medicine was soothing. She held on to the empty mug, somehow gathering strength from the feel of it, and told them of her first encounter with Jack Bowman.

"Now he's come!" she finished. "I have seen him. He has come to take us back, and you'll all be punished, does he find us here!"

She looked from one to another for blame or for comfort, but her tears blurred their faces. No one spoke. Pearl could hardly bear their silence.

At last Matill said, "We have walked for days, all unaware of this fellow. He'll not be traveling alone. There will be others with him. Had they recognized you, they could have challenged us anywhere along the way."

"Of course!" Will agreed. "He has come to the fair on some errand of his own, or of Sir Geoffrey's."

"And he would never know you now with that cropped hair," Joan said. "You met him but the once before."

There was a low growl from Rob. He pointed at Pearl, at Gavin, at his own tongueless mouth. He tried to speak. Gruff, hollow sounds came from deep in his throat. Pearl had never seen Rob like this. Always his smile and his eyes had done his speaking. This awful voice without a tongue shocked and sickened her. Yet at once she felt ashamed of her feelings.

Rob's outburst had startled everyone. Widsith, who was standing next to him, threw an arm across his shoulders. "Right you are, old friend," he said gently. "These two shall never suffer as you have done. We'll not let them go back to their master and be punished. You have my word on it!"

Gavin raised a hand to silence him. "You risk too much for us. Pearl and I had best go our own way."

"Pah!" said Matill. "Were we afraid of risk, we'd not have taken you with us to begin with. Of course you'll stay! What say the rest of you?"

"Aye," answered Will and Joan together.

"That settles it," said Widsith. He took his flute from his belt—people were approaching the wagon in anticipation of the next performance. "Gavin, you and Pearl wait out of sight amongst those trees till we're done."

They left Greencastle in the rain, which had begun to fall

during the night. Already the road was a muddy stream washing over deep ruts. Only Garth rode in the wagon, with Tom Pilgrim at the reins.

The rest slipped and slid through the muck. They huddled deep into their cloaks against the chill wind, their hoods pulled far forward. Beads of water bounced onto the oiled cloth stretched over the wagon.

The foul weather matched their mood. All last evening Gavin had tried to persuade Pearl to run away with him. The others would not hear of it, and Pearl did not want to go. They had all gone to bed at cross-purposes with one another. This morning, waking to rain in wet blankets, they had had little to say while Widsith hitched Mule to the wagon.

"Surely you must see that my way is best," Gavin argued now, as Pearl stopped to pull a twig from between her toes. Like the others, she had put her shoes in the wagon. "If the bowman has already discovered us, he'll run from fair to fair looking for us. But do we stay behind at the next town—well, he'll not expect that. We'll be safe then. One year in a town and we are free from all masters!"

Pearl would not listen. She felt she would be safer with the troupe than on the run with only Gavin for company. "Besides," she said, "town life is not for me. Oh, Gavin, with the troupe I can learn to be a minstrel! The thought takes hold of my heart and sets it singing. 'Tis worth almost any risk."

Gavin's only reply was a scowl.

Up ahead, the wagon tilted sideways. One of the wheels had sunk to its hub in the mud. They all pushed and tugged so Mule could pull it free. Exhausted from their efforts, they stopped to rest and eat. The rain continued to drench them. Wet, wind-tossed leaves clung to their hair and their cloaks.

They spent the night in a hermit's hut, curled close to his fire on the dirt floor. The steaming odor of their wet clothes mingled with that of boiled leeks and turnips. For most of the night the rain dripped through a gap in the roof. Its plop-plopping into a wooden bucket finally lulled them to sleep.

The bright sun was drying up the puddles in the road when they bade the hermit farewell. Their next stop would be Bristol, where Gavin planned to leave them.

As they walked, Widsith tried to discourage him. "A man who lacks gainful work lacks welcome in a town. You have no way to earn your keep, Gavin."

"I can learn a trade," Gavin insisted. "I can be an armorer, or a blacksmith."

"Lad, lad," Widsith sighed, "you be ill-prepared for town life. You can learn no trade unless you are apprenticed to a master in it. To be 'prenticed you must be known to the master who will teach you. And you must be fourteen years old, besides!"

Only Will seemed to understand Gavin's need. "Let the boy make his own way, does he want to," he chided Widsith.

To Gavin he said, "You might try chance work. It be only a sometime thing, doing whatever work chances your way. Giving a hand to one craftsman or another. Any sort of mean work too low for a skilled man, and which a busy 'prentice has no time for."

Gavin's face brightened. "There's the remedy, Will! I'll do chance work till I find a master who will apprentice me when

I come of age. You can do that, too, Pearl! You can do chance work for someone like Gwen Weaver."

Pearl almost hated Will for showing Gavin a way. Yet she knew Gavin was set on leaving.

"Nay, brother," she said, "though parting from you will sorely grieve me. We've lived our whole lives together! But these good friends want me to stay. And I have already apprenticed myself— to Matill Makejoye!"

It was true. She longed to be everything Matill was. Strong and brave. True to a talent that gave joy to oneself and pleasure to others. Never mind if the future held a few rotten eggs. She smiled shyly up at Matill.

"And I'm proud to have such an apprentice," Matill said in a voice that told Pearl she really meant it. Her quick response made Pearl resolve to put aside her fears.

My name is Pearl in the Egg, and I'm going to be a minstrel! she told herself joyously. She began to sing.

> "Though the sun be fierce or the wind be strong,
>   Come hither, come hither, and follow my song,
>   Which beckons and beckons, now low, now loud,
>   As the white dust blows in a swirling cloud."

Will joined in, then Matill. Soon they were all singing as they trailed the wagon. They approached some travelers who had stopped at the side of the road to rest. Pearl looked them over quickly. Peddlers, she judged, from their dress and their pack mules.

For a few tense moments she thought that one was not. He

stood in the shadow of a tree, leaning against the trunk, a flask to his lips. Her blood pounded as they drew nearer. She knew she should hide her face, yet her eyes were drawn to him.

Her breath caught. Not Jack, but a stranger! Still, she stared at him as they passed. *The fellow will think I am daft,* she thought, and giggled.

"What's so funny?" Widsith asked.

Pearl's sudden relief made her giddy. She could not stop the silly giggling.

Widsith made a sign with his finger to his head. "Daft," he said to the others.

Pearl laughed until the tears came.

They looked for Jack Bowman in Bristol, but saw no sign of him. "He has taken another road, Pearl," Widsith assured her. "Whatever his business, it has nothing to do with you."

Pearl let herself be persuaded. She took her turn on the stage with the others. But Gavin would not. He shook his head when Matill came to him about it. They would soon have to do without him anyway.

Before they left Bristol, Will found a place for Gavin to stay. A pork butcher would let the boy sleep in his shop if he would clean out the butchering shed every day. It was bloody work, but Gavin accepted it eagerly.

Widsith held his nose. "Surely a juggler's work is not such an insult to the nostrils as this!" he joked.

But Gavin paid no heed to the teasing. However foul the shed smelled, the town air was sweet.

It came time to leave. One by one they wished Gavin Godspeed. Pearl kissed him, then turned away to hide her tears.

"Never mind," Matill said as Tom Pilgrim got the wagon moving. "He'll be glad to come back to us when we return next year."

"And we'll be glad to have him—after he takes a bath in strong lye soap!" Widsith quipped, trying to make Pearl laugh. Her weak smile was poor reward.

Rob came to walk beside her. She found his nearness comforting, yet she could only be cheered for the moment. She might never see Gavin again. At the next town Jack Bowman could be waiting.

ELEVEN

THE GIFT

GAVIN WAS GONE, and now there was to be yet another parting. Tom Pilgrim was nearly recovered, and bound for a monastery a day's journey from Bristol.

"As I left on my pilgrimage," he had told them, "I vowed, for my safe return, to enter this monastery of Black Friars." They had promised to take him there.

It was not quite dusk when the square stone buildings appeared, huddled against a hillside behind a wall of stone and earth. Tom stopped Mule at the gatehouse and jumped down to pull on the bell rope.

The Brother Porter raised the wicket and peered out, blinking. "Yes, what is it?"

"Travelers begging a night's rest," said Tom. "I have business with the Father Abbot on the morrow."

The Brother Porter took note of Tom's robe and of his holy-shrine tokens. For the rest he had only a twitch of his nose. He caught sight of Garth and shuddered.

"*You* may go on into the main building. Supper will be served in the refectory," he told Tom. "There is room in the gatehouse for the women. These—" he sniffed and waved his hand at the men standing alongside the wagon—"these can eat in the kitchen and bed down there."

"I will eat and sleep with my friends," Tom said. His tone matched the disdain in the porter's voice. "Ladies, I will return in the morning to wish you Godspeed."

The porter slammed the wicket shut. He came to the gate with the key and a rushlight. He opened the gate and Tom drove the wagon into the courtyard.

As the men went off toward the kitchen, the porter led the women through a door on the other side of the court. In the unsteady glow of the rushlight their shadows bobbed up and down on the stone walls of a narrow passage. They could hear the monks chanting plainsong in the distance.

The porter stopped at a low door and opened it onto a small square room where several pallets were neatly stacked in a corner.

He set the rushlight into a wall bracket, then looked down his long nose at them and sniffed again. "Those pallets are not of common straw, as you are accustomed to, but of the finest goose feathers. And they are free of lice, so see that you leave none behind you!"

Later, a brother tapped on the door and left them a trencher of turnips and two loaves of fresh, warm bread. When they had finished eating, Joan set the trencher back in the hall outside the door. She flopped down on her pallet with a contented sigh. Matill blew out the light.

Pearl could not sleep; she tossed restlessly on the unfamiliar feathers. They smelled musty and damp. She would have much preferred a bed of fresh, sweet straw.

Thoughts of Gavin and Jack Bowman came crowding into her mind. She lay wakeful until dawn.

Just as they were about to leave, Tom Pilgrim came to see them off. He brought his harp.

"This, for you," he said to Pearl. "My holy vows will not permit me to own such a thing in this place. But I rejoice that it will be in your keeping."

Pearl stared, unbelieving, from Tom to the harp.

Joan gave her a gentle shove. "Be you daft, girl? 'Tis a gift. Take it!"

Pearl took the harp and held it close. "Th-thank you, dear Tom! Always when I play it I will think of you."

Tom smiled with gentle sadness. "Play it now, as you go. And sing! I will hear you both for one last time."

Widsith was already at the reins. Pearl climbed into the wagon and they started out, the sweet music and song drifting over the courtyard behind them.

> "Let us sing of bright morn breaking
>   Over purple dells;
> Lilies fair their sheaths forsaking;
> Larks in light their music making;
> Sing the song of wings and waking
>   Over our farewells!"

The gate closed behind them. Pearl's voice broke. How bitter-sweet life was! Joy and sorrow mixed together, following one upon the other time and again. She laid the harp aside. No need to spoil its silken strings with tears.

When they reached the main road again, Pearl took Garth into the wagon. She had decided to teach him to dance to her harping. At first he watched with mild curiosity, his head cocked to one side. But he behaved the way Mule did sometimes, and would not budge.

"Come on, Garth," she coaxed. "See how it's done? First one foot, then the other." To her delight, he finally tried to mimic her.

Rob, who had watched with amusement, came to the wagon to show her how to rub Garth's stomach to reward his efforts. They smiled at each other, seeing that the monkey was as pleased with himself as they were with him.

Their last stop before London was the three-day fair at Reading. By the time they arrived, Garth could dance to most of "The Wandering Song." There was still no sign of Jack Bowman, and Pearl's fears were lulled. She took her turn on the stage, this time without any prodding from Matill. Her harping had much improved with the long hours of practice since they had left the monastery. She was eager to test herself in front of an audience.

Pearl brought Garth onto the stage and set him to dancing while she played and sang. Immediately they caught the crowd's fancy. She heard cries of, "Look! Come see! 'Tis a girl minstrel with a monkey!"

Again and again Pearl and Garth were brought back for more.

Finally Garth sat down in the middle of his dance and would not get up again. Pearl's efforts to prod him brought a roar of sympathetic laughter and shouts of, "Enough! The monk has earned his rest!"

Later, they watched as Matill counted the money. "Look at it all!" she exclaimed. "Never have we taken in so much on one fair day! And we have two more days in Reading."

"Let's celebrate," said Widsith. "Wait till I move Mule to a new patch of grass. Then we can stroll around and take in some of the fair ourselves."

But Joan said she was tired, to Widsith's obvious disappointment. Matill had torn the hem of her dress and wanted to mend it before dark. Pearl decided to remain behind with them. Will and Rob were ready to accompany Widsith. When Garth saw them leaving, he flitted about, chattering with indecision. Finally he leaped onto Pearl's shoulder and scolded the departing Rob.

"Widsith!" Matill called. She threw him a small purse. "Get some salt fish for the morning meal."

Pearl reached for her harp and climbed onto the wagon seat to try out a new song. Behind her, Joan sighed and leaned against the seat, listening. Matill pulled her mending box out from under the wagon and sat on a chest with her dress pulled around so she could catch up the hem.

"Listen to this," Pearl said after a while. "See how you like my new song." She strummed the harp a few times and began to sing:

> "As I was going down to Derby
>   Once upon a market day,
>   I saw the biggest ram, sir,
>   That ever fed on hay.

"The ram was fat behind, sir,
The ram was fat before—"

Pearl stopped abruptly.

"Oh, do go on, love," urged Matill. "That song promises to be a comical one. The folk will—" She glanced up to see Pearl's stiffened form and a broad-shouldered man swaggering toward them.

"That's he?" she whispered. When Pearl nodded, Matill shook Joan awake. "Psst! The bowman comes!"

Joan's eyes flew open. She sat straight up.

The man drew near, smiling them a greeting and tipping up his empty flask. "Now, don't I be the lucky fellow?" he said. "I swig down the last drop of ale just as I come upon three pretty maids all alone! What say you we all go to the brewster's booth and remedy the situation?"

"I think not," Matill answered sharply. "We are tired and want to take our ease."

He rubbed his nose and eyed Pearl's harp with interest. "Pearl in the Egg. Do I have the name right? You have a curious instrument there."

Pearl's fingers tightened on the harp. Garth reached down and took the man's empty flask.

"You—you saw us perform today, then?" Joan asked. "You know our names. What do you call yourself?"

"Aye, I saw you, and Jack's my name. I'm bowman to Sir Geoffrey of Landsford, though the errand he sends me on takes other skills."

"Which you have, of course," said Matill.

He laughed. "Which I have. Come, now. 'Tis a rare treat to meet lady minstrels! If you won't let me buy you an ale, how about sharing some of yours with me?"

"We have only cider, and not overmuch of it," Joan told him.

He laughed again and snatched his flask back from Garth. "That's quite a monkey," he said to Pearl. "You led him a merry dance today with your music."

Still Pearl did not speak. Jack peered at her through narrowed eyes. "There be a familiar look to you. Something close-up that I didn't catch watching you perform. Have we met before? When you had longer hair, perhaps? What happened to your hair?"

"Fever!" Joan almost shouted. "She's had the fever."

Jack's eyes widened in mock horror. "And does the fever keep the maid from answering for her own self? She has a voice, I know, for she sang right well not an hour ago." He reached out to touch Pearl's hair.

"Leave hold!" Pearl cried. She pushed his hand away and slid across the seat. Startled, Garth leaped to the ground and ran screeching under the wagon.

Pearl's cry and Garth's shrieks were answered by a bellow from Rob as he raced toward them. A single blow sent Jack spinning in one direction, his flask in another. He staggered, righted himself, and stared stupidly at Rob.

Will and Widsith arrived on the run, to stand on either side of Rob.

"Best you be off about your business," Widsith said quietly, "else you will get more of the same."

Still looking bewildered, Jack picked up his flask and rubbed his jaw with it. "N-no harm," he stammered. "I meant no harm.

Just trying to place where I'd seen the girl." He waited for some reply. When none came, he shrugged, turned on his heel, and sauntered off.

They watched him leave. "He spoke the truth, I think," Joan said. "He really meant no harm." She turned to Pearl. "You'll get used to his sort, love. When some men drink, they chase after women in a rude manner. 'Tis just a part of life on the road."

But when Widsith heard who it was they had just driven off, he was not so sure. "That one will not soon forget the feel of Rob's knuckles on his jaw," he said.

Matill was quick to get the point. "And remembering the sting of that, he'll soon enough get around to remembering how he came to know Pearl!"

Widsith nodded grimly.

Rob looked stricken. He gave an anguished moan and hid his face in his arms.

"We'd best leave this place," Will said.

"We can give up these next two fair days and go straight to London," Widsith suggested. "'Tis home to us, and crowded enough for Pearl to go unnoticed. This was our last stop before London anyway."

"I can't let you give up the money from two fair days!" Pearl cried. "Gavin was right. I should have gone with him."

Matill waved her silent and looked at Widsith. "We have money enough to get through the winter, I think—unless spring delays its coming."

Widsith nodded and went at once to get the wagon slats. Will and Rob helped him set them up in place.

It was nearly dark when they finished loading the wagon.

No one traveled the roads after sunset.

"We will leave at first light," Widsith said. "The bowman won't miss us till fair time, and by then we'll be well on our way."

They settled down to a restless sleep. Pearl was sure she did not close her eyes once during the long night. Toward dawn she heard Rob moaning and weeping. She got up to go to him. She saw Widsith sitting alone in the wagon, keeping watch.

She knelt beside Rob and held his hand till he slept again.

TWELVE

LONDON

IN SPITE of their fears, the trip to London was uneventful. They arrived on a cold October afternoon under a sky the dull gray of undyed wool. The smell of coming winter hung on the air. They took their turn in line with the other traffic streaming through Newgate in the great wall surrounding the city.

"Hold your nose!" Joan said. "The butchers all have their shops nearby."

"And watch where you walk," Widsith warned. He pointed to a gutter in the middle of the cobbled street. It was full of the waste from slaughtered animals, and worse.

Suddenly Will grabbed Pearl's arm and pulled her close to the wall of a shop. "Watch above as well as below!" he shouted. From a window overhead a bucket of slops missed the gutter by an arm's length and splattered at their feet.

They walked along the river, where barges, ferryboats, and

smaller craft darted about. Pearl gasped at a near miss when three boats nearly collided.

She stopped to admire a sailing ship at anchor. She wondered how it felt to trust oneself on the sea to this frail-looking thing of wood and canvas.

But of all the strange, new things, Pearl thought the window places in the houses were the greatest marvel. These were not mere holes in the wall that had to be shuttered against the weather. Instead, they were fitted with small squares of polished horn that let in light as they kept out cold!

The din was enough to set Pearl's ears buzzing. Boatmen bawled out warnings to one another. Peddlers bellowed their wares. Beggars whined for alms and called down curses on those who passed by with upturned noses and unloosened purse strings. There were small children begging. Pearl remembered the day in Wat's wagon when Diccon Tollman had said that she and Gavin might fall in with a beggar and become cutpurses. She wondered if any of these children were runaways in the hands of cruel new masters.

It was quiet in Kitchen Lane. Matill stopped at a door in the long row of houses. She lifted a heavy brass knocker and let it fall with a clang against the plate behind it. While they waited, Widsith drove on with the wagon through an alley alongside the house.

The door swung open on its leather hinges. A tall man as thin as an ox rib looked out at them. His long white hair fell loosely around the collar of his faded brown shirt. Small splotches of purple dotted his wrinkled face.

His gaze went from Pearl, with Garth on her shoulder, to Matill, standing beside her. At sight of his daughter, his dull brown eyes warmed with pleasure. His pale lips turned up in a smile of welcome.

"Well, Fa," Matill said, "we've come home for the winter, with yet another mouth to feed." She grinned at Pearl. "We call her Pearl in the Egg, and she's a minstrel."

The old man's smile widened. He took Pearl's hand and drew her into the house. "'Tis a sweet face under that ill-cut hair," he said. "Welcome, welcome!"

When Pearl awoke the next morning, she did not know where she was. Instead of the high arc of sky above, there was a close darkness slanting downward almost to her feet. With her hands she felt beneath the thick layer of straw and touched wooden planks. Beside her, Joan stretched and yawned and sat up, scratching. From below she heard footsteps.

Then Pearl remembered. She was in the sleeping loft above the single room in Matill's father's house. She was in London!

Joan stood up and yawned again. "Let's find something to eat before we starve!"

They crawled down the ladder to the floor below. Matill's father was there, eating cold griddle cakes.

"Fa Roger," Joan said, "surely you're not going a-begging to-day! We have just come from six good months on the road. Rest for a time. At least till our purse runs dry!"

He shook his head. "I'll go till the cold drives me in. The winter may be longer than we think."

Matill had come down the ladder. She went to her father and kissed him lightly on the cheek. "Go along, Fa. The dogs and pigs and even some of the gentles would wonder, did you miss out on a good day."

He stuffed a griddle cake into his worn pouch and went to the door. "And a good day it is. See that sunrise!" The door closed. They heard his footsteps fading away.

Matill sighed. "Fa has lived too long. He's old and can no longer go a-trouping. Age has stiffened his fingers. He can no longer play his music, and he knows no other trade. He belongs to no craftsman's guild for help in his olden years. Yet he must eat! He needs a roof to keep out the weather, a fire against the chill.

"Such will our lot be, when we grow old. But enough of that!" She sat down and patted the bench beside her.

Pearl took the place Matill indicated, suddenly aware of her hunger. The men appeared, looking to see what there was to eat.

Matill spread dripping on a cake. She rolled it up and bit off half. "Today we go to Smithfield," she said with her mouth full, "to lay in food for the winter."

Widsith ticked off on his fingers: "Turnips, salt pork, onions. Perhaps some raisins and dates?"

Matill nodded. "And Pearl needs new harp strings. Tomorrow we'll call on the silk merchant."

"We need new clothes for next year's trouping," Joan reminded her.

"All in good time," Matill said, chewing. "After Smithfield."

Smithfield, Joan explained as they made ready to leave, was a large marketplace outside the walls of London. "Filled with marvelous treats from all over the world!"

Now that Pearl was safely inside a house again, she did not want to leave. Reluctantly she gave in to Matill's assurance that

Jack Bowman would be hard put to find her here, even if he came so far looking for her.

"Did he even come, he would not stay," Will said. "The roads all bog down in winter, and Sir Geoffrey will want him home. He'll need his bowman more than he'll need a runaway."

There was no sign of Jack Bowman at Smithfield, nor at any of the other places in the city where they went. But it was only after the cold winter rains shut them all indoors that Pearl felt truly safe.

She could relax at last, and enjoy the quiet companionship of her new life. They spent the days close to the fire on the hearthstone, roasting chestnuts or taking turns stirring the stew-pot and getting to sniff the savory steam rising from it. At night they warmed stones to carry up to the sleeping loft. They took turns braving the weather to see to Mule in the shed behind the house.

Pearl watched Widsith and Joan making double duty of this task, and shivered. When it was the turn of one of them to tend Mule, they both went. They seemed not to mind the cold and the wet, but to welcome the chance to be alone together. Sometimes they took warm stones to the loft and remained there long after the stones had cooled, talking in lowered voices and laughing a lot.

Matill had put everyone to work stitching new leggings and shirts for the men, new dresses and shifts for the women. To the dresses Joan added bits of ribbon and a few glass beads for trimming.

Their old cloaks would do them, Matill decided, except for

Rob's, which was worn too thin in places. "A new cloak for Rob," she said with a careful counting of coins. "His old one can go for patches."

"Give that to me," Joan said. "Widsith's cloak needs a new hood." She snipped the old hood from Widsith's cloak and measured out a new one from a piece of Rob's. When the new hood was almost finished, she took two dark green rosemary leaves from her herb box. She tucked them carefully into the hem and stitched it shut.

"To keep him true to me," Joan explained to Pearl.

Pearl found a coverchief thrown into the pile of mending scraps. She folded it and cut a small hole in the center. She took Garth up to the loft.

"Be still, now, Garth," she commanded as the monkey wriggled and chattered. For answer, he threw his arms around her and gave her a kiss. She pried him loose and pulled the coverchief over his head, belting it around his middle with some twisted yarn.

She brought him back downstairs and set him on his feet. Humming a tune, she took his hand and danced a few steps. Obedient for once, he danced with her.

Joan looked up from the ribbon she was measuring. "Oh, look! Garth in a tunic! Pearl, how clever."

Pearl spent long hours practicing and composing new songs. Once she overheard Matill saying to her father, "The girl is gifted, Fa. She has taken to music like a bird to flight. Have you ever heard a truer voice?"

Fa Roger vowed he had not, and Pearl added pride of accomplishment to her new sense of well-being.

"My name is Pearl in the Egg and I really *am* a minstrel!" she whispered to Garth.

She composed several winter songs, but there was one that especially appealed to Fa Roger:

> "I have heard—I don't know whether
>   Wide awake or fast asleep—
> That the stars once sang together
>   To some shepherds tending sheep.
>
> "So, at night, when they are glistening,
>   Just before I close my eyes,
> I look up, and keep a-listening
>   For the music from the skies."

Gradually the days grew shorter, then began to lengthen again. The longer days brought warmer weather. One afternoon Will went out to Newgate and returned with the news that the roads were fit for travel.

"Good," said Widsith. "We leave tomorrow." His words earned him a chorus of cheers. They spent the rest of the day in preparation.

Pearl watched Fa Roger putting Garth through his steps. Another parting! She felt saddened to be leaving the old man behind. She glanced up to see Matill watching him, too. Tears shimmered in Matill's eyes.

Sleep was hard to come by that night. Pearl lay in the loft listening to the watchman calling out the hours, one by one. But shortly before dawn she dozed. When Matill shook her awake she saw daylight spilling through the small loft window.

They ate, though Pearl scarcely touched her food. Widsith brought the wagon around to the street door. Fa Roger came outside to see them off.

"Mind me well, Fa," Matill told him, "and take care. Stay at home when the weather is bad." She pressed a small purse into his hand.

He tried to give it back. "You have six to feed, and Garth as well. I'll not need this."

Matill shook her head, dislodging a tear, which splashed down her cheek and onto her hand. She tried to speak, and could not.

"Take it, Fa," said Widsith. He clapped the old man on the shoulder, then turned sharply and led the way up the street.

Rob and Garth followed Widsith in the wagon. The others trailed behind. Matill looked back and waved. "Each spring it gets harder to leave him here," she sighed.

Their mood brightened as they joined other groups passing through the gate. The sun shone warmly behind the morning mist. A light breeze carried the scent of early flowers and budding bushes. The road stretched out ahead of them for as far as they could see.

Softly Pearl began to sing. Presently the others joined in. Jack Bowman was forgotten. It was spring, and Pearl in the Egg was starting out on her very first long tour as a minstrel.

THIRTEEN

RESCUE

HE TROUPE had cause to be proud of Pearl. At every performance the crowds kept calling her back. She played until she was sore-fingered, sang until her throat was dry. Finally Widsith had to step in and make them release her. They cheered all the more as, flushed with success, she made her final bows.

While all the troupe rejoiced with Pearl, Matill was the proudest. She had, after all, sensed Pearl's talent right from the start, goading the girl on whenever she faltered.

"See! See!" Matill would say, counting money and pointing to gifts of food at the end of a fair day. "We have always brought one another goodwill and good fortune. Now Pearl brings us more of it!"

Pearl smilingly accepted the praise, knowing all the while what goodwill and good fortune they brought her.

On leaving Winchester, the wagon broke an axle and they had to go back. The delay cost them two days. By the time they reached Shaftesbury, the fair was on. As they entered the fairground, their attention was drawn to a crowd gathered at a wagon to watch a sour-faced man and a short, scrawny girl.

The girl was younger than Pearl. She stood with head hung low, shoulders hunched forward, hands clenched tightly at her sides.

"What am I offered for this fine young maid?" the man was saying. "Come, gentle men and gentle ladies! Here be an able acrobat to add to the merriment of your guests. Show the gentles what you can do, my Helsa!"

He poked the child so rudely that she swayed and nearly lost her balance. But she obeyed his command. She raised her head, stretched her arms high, and threw herself into handsprings around the stage. She righted herself, sat down with her wrists locked around her ankles, and rolled over and over, like a hoop. She untangled her arms and legs and stood again, touching the toe of first one foot and then the other to her forehead.

The man signaled her to stop and stepped forward to lead the applause.

"Did I hear a sum mentioned here?" He crooked his hand hornlike over his ear and bent down to listen as someone repeated an offer.

"Well, now, I'm sorry, sir," he replied, straightening up again and speaking loudly for the benefit of all. "This child is worth a great deal more, as I'm sure you'll agree. Who else? Who will add this marvel to their household today?"

Pearl stared, openmouthed. "Is that terrible man really going to sell that little girl?" she demanded of Matill. "Sell his own child?"

Matill shrugged. "Likely she's not his, but an orphan or runaway. A waif with nowhere to go. He has thrown her a few morsels to eat and given her a bundle of rags for a bed, and now he wants his reward."

"Can't *we* buy her?" Pearl begged. "Oh, please, Matill! She will be safe with us and will get us back her price in good time. Folk will pay to see her do all those clever things."

Matill shook her head. "I understand how you feel, Pearl. But you will see more of this, and worse, as we go. We can't take in every waif we see."

Pearl turned away from Matill and reached for her harp bag. She snatched the harp free and ran with it to the man's wagon, shoving people out of her way.

She glared up into the man's hostile eyes. "I have barter here, sir. This grand harp, made in faraway Burma, be yours for the maid. The harp, sir, is of rare design. See! You'll not find another like it in England."

The fellow gaped at her in surprise. Then he made a great show of rude laughter. "A harp, now! And what am I to do with that? Am I a gleeman? I'd be put to the bother of selling it, when I've trouble enough to get this off my hands." Again he jabbed at Helsa.

Suddenly something flew through the air over the heads of those nearest the wagon and landed with a jangle at the man's feet. It was a lady's purse, of yellow silk with a flower design pricked out in gold thread.

Pearl looked around to see a fair-haired young woman astride a gray pony. Her gown was of the same stuff as the purse.

Her pony's saddle was gilt-edged and richly embroidered. Behind her, on horseback, were several men and women as grand as herself. She stared at Helsa's captor with contempt in her blue eyes.

"Take the purse, lout! And send the girl to me." She pointed a gloved hand at Pearl. "Come, both of you."

"Now there be a gentle with a kind thought for the misfortunate!" a woman screamed.

"Aye," shouted another. "God bless you, lady!" Others took up the cry, although until this moment no one had thought to care about what happened to Helsa.

"Don't be frightened," the woman said to Helsa, who stood pale and shaken beside the pony. To Pearl she said, "You are a brave girl, and a generous one. There is place for you both in my household, if you will come with me."

Pearl's eyes widened. Here was a gentle taking notice of her, wanting her. But she said only, "Take Helsa, my lady, please! As for me, I cannot." She saw Widsith and Matill elbowing their way toward her.

The woman followed her glance and beckoned them forward. "Surely these are not your parents? They look so young."

"Oh, no, my lady. Of parents I have none. But these have snatched me from a dreadful fate, as you have done for Helsa. They have taken me into their troupe of entertainers. I will stay with them, though I thank you for your kindness."

"A troupe! You are a troupe?" The woman's eyes sparkled with interest. "I am Lady Hythe," she said to Matill, who had just reached them, all out of breath, with Widsith close behind. "You are performing here today?"

"Y-yes, m-my lady," Matill answered. "We have only to un-
pack our gear and set up for it."

"Then I shall return to watch. Helsa, too. I think perhaps
you can do me a service." She signaled one of the men to take
Helsa up behind him on his mount.

Helsa still clung to Pearl's hand with cold fingers. "Thank
you!" she murmured. "You have been the saving of me! Were
it not for your—"

"Come, Helsa," Lady Hythe said gently. "You two will see
each other later on, I promise." She guided her pony away
through the crowd. Her friends followed. Helsa held on to the
horseman with one hand and waved to Pearl with the other.

The troupe prepared for their first performance at Shaftesbury
with great excitement and much speculation about what service
Lady Hythe might call upon them to perform.

Matill dashed about making suggestions so that they all might
make their best impression. "Garth must dance in his tunic,"
she told Rob. "But let him first walk the rope so he will be
fresh for that, and not fall and hurt himself.

To Pearl she said, "Save for last those songs which you have
composed yourself. They are the best, after all."

Rob pointed at Pearl, then in the direction Lady Hythe had
taken. He grinned, and made as if to play on a harp.

"Aye, Rob," Matill said with a wry smile. "Our Pearl has
caught the eye of a gentle—and sooner even than I thought.
Now, hear me, Pearl. Do your best to please my lady!"

Pearl did not reply. She would do her best, but she was not
going to leave the troupe for any gentle.

When all was ready, Widsith called the folk together with

his flute. Lady Hythe came with her friends and Helsa. Some in the crowd recognized them now, and made way.

Matill was first to perform. The others followed in turn, until it was time for Pearl and Garth, then Pearl alone. With much pride Widsith announced each of the songs she had composed herself. As at other performances, the applause continued until she would sing yet another.

Finally, seeing that Widsith was about to call an end to it, she said, laughing, "This be my last song for now! 'Tis one of my own, and a favorite of a very dear friend." She sang the winter song Fa Roger loved.

It was over. The crowd had gone. Only Lady Hythe and her company remained. Helsa ran to Pearl and hugged her.

"Never have I been so entertained," said Lady Hythe. "Not only do you each work well, but you all work well together. Such fine comradeship pleases me more than you know."

She turned to Pearl. "And you, child, are as musically gifted as you are generous and brave!"

"Thank you, my lady," Pearl murmured, flushing. The others echoed her.

"Tell me," Lady Hythe said to Widsith, "do you know where Swindon manor is? Can you come there one day soon?"

"Aye, my lady," Widsith said. "'Tis not far off the London road. We go that way in three months' time."

"Then come to me there. Swindon is my home," she explained. "I am only visiting here. I would like you to entertain some very special guests. I will pay you well for your trouble. And—" her smile turned mysterious—"if you are willing, I may have an important mission for you as well."

She left soon after, with their eager promise to come to Swindon.

"My lady is childless," Pearl told them later. "Helsa told me. She takes in waifs, who work for her in exchange for their keep. And she will have no serfs on her land! Only freemen and women, who work for pay or for goods of value."

"She has no husband, then?" asked Joan.

"Gone on Crusade," Pearl said. "Lady Hythe stays behind to manage the manor house and lands."

"What 'important mission' can she have in mind for us?" Will wondered aloud.

They all wondered. It would make conversation for many an evening around their fire.

FOURTEEN

DISASTER

THEY CAME to a crossroad. To the left lay Wallbrooke Town. To the right was a smaller town where the troupe had played only once. Its market days were poorly attended, so they had never returned. Now, however, this place was their destination. Pearl felt a pang of regret that she would not see Gwen and Wat; that the troupe must do without the extra money that Wallbrooke would bring them. Yet they dared not take the risk. They turned to the right.

They had not gone far when they heard horses overtaking them. Those on foot leaped nimbly aside into the fields. Rob pulled the wagon off the road just as four mounted men galloped up from behind. Three wore the black and yellow livery of some noble lord. The fourth was more grandly dressed, in yellow hose and a green tunic.

Joan coughed out a mouthful of dust. Garth screamed as he

always did when they stopped to make way for other travelers. With a stifled cry Pearl dropped down behind the wagon.

"Holy saints!" Matill muttered. "Did I see Jack?"

Pearl nodded. She ran her tongue over dry lips. "And Sir Geoffrey, in the green."

They all stared at each other, wondering what to do. Was it safe to turn around and go to Wallbrooke? Or might Sir Geoffrey return while they were there, perhaps even stop by at one of their performances? The road to his manor house led straight through the center of town.

Yet there was also great danger in following Sir Geoffrey's party on to the next town. The safest course was to avoid both towns—but this would bring them to Greencastle two weeks before fair time.

Widsith had carefully mapped out the route they traveled each year from London and back to take advantage of the best fairs and market days in towns all along the way. The coming winter would be a lean one if no money came in from now until the fair at Greencastle.

"Let's go on," Widsith said at last. "We will camp outside town. Then Will and I can try to find out if Sir Geoffrey is staying there, or has only passed through."

They went on, anxiously alert for the sound of returning hoof-beats, until Mule suddenly halted at a turn in the road. He sniffed the air and brayed. Will dashed ahead to look for the cause of the beast's alarm.

He returned, plainly agitated. "Sir Geoffrey's party!" he said. "Highwaymen have ambushed them. They lie in the ditch and their horses are gone. Mule smells blood!"

"Dead?" asked Widsith.

"Not all. I heard groans."

Joan hurried to the wagon for her herb box.

"What are you doing?" Matill called after her. "We should keep on going whilst we still can! Let someone else find them."

"Oh, Matill!" Pearl cried. "They need our help!"

"And *you* need to be found out, I suppose?" Matill snapped. She put her hands on her hips and glared around at them all. She saw distress in Pearl's eyes, accusation in Joan's. She looked to the men for approval. Only Rob offered any. Widsith and Will looked uneasy and doubtful.

Widsith turned to Pearl. "'Tis for you to say," he told her gently. "But, Pearl, you have much to lose! Better we should do as Matill says."

Pearl's gaze did not waver. "I say we help them." The words sounded brave, but she was terrified. She was risking all to save the life of her enemy.

Pearl squared her shoulders and started toward the bend in the road. The others followed, Matill complaining all the way, Rob leading the reluctant Mule.

They scrambled down into the ditch where the men lay sprawled. The robbers had cut the pouches from their belts and ripped their clothes in a search for money and other valuables.

Will crouched down near the first man. "Dead," he said, getting to his feet again.

Someone groaned. It was Jack Bowman. The right shoulder of his tunic was soaked with blood. Joan knelt to examine him.

"A deep knife wound. Clear to the bone, I think."

Blood seeped through the front of Sir Geoffrey's green tunic. He did not appear to be breathing. Widsith put his ear near the red stain, then nodded to Joan. "He lives."

The fourth man lay on his stomach. Gently Will and Widsith rolled him over. One eye stared up at them. The other was lost beneath a great bloody lump.

"Dead," Will pronounced a second time.

"Wait," said Widsith. "See, he blinks! He has been stupefied by the blow to his head."

Pearl spread blankets out on the ground near each of the wounded men while Rob cleared space for them in the wagon. Matill pulled old shifts from a chest and tore them into bandages. She took them to Joan and helped her stop the bleeding and bind up the wounds.

Widsith and Will began digging a grave for the dead man. "Turn the wagon around," Widsith said to Rob. "We had best leave them with the sheriff at Wallbrooke. He can get word to the manor house. Whether these fellows live or die, they will want to be as near to home as can be."

When the earth was heaped back over the grave, they gently lifted the wounded onto the blankets, then into the wagon. Joan climbed in after them. Rob took up the reins.

Matill frowned at Pearl as they walked behind. "At least pin up your hair!" she scolded, grabbing Pearl by the arm. "'Tis all grown out again, you know!" She pulled off her coverchief and took pins from her own hair. She twisted Pearl's in a loop, pinned it up, and tied on the coverchief.

Joan called to her. The motion of the wagon on the rough road had started the wounds bleeding again. "Help me," she said. "I need more bandages, and someone must see to them whilst I mix more of this salve. 'Tis the one thing that will keep them from bleeding to death."

Matill climbed into the wagon. When Pearl would have followed, Matill pushed her back. "Stay at a distance. There is no room up here for you anyway."

They made camp a half day's journey from Wallbrooke. Joan, looking exhausted, stood at the fire eating a hasty meal. Pearl went to fetch her a mug of cider.

Jack Bowman had revived somewhat and had managed to prop himself up. He moaned and cursed, looking dully around to see where he was. Pearl gasped and turned away, spilling the cider.

Startled, Joan said, "I'll take him something to eat and make him lie down again."

Sir Geoffrey had rallied, too, and tried to sit up. "Let me tend to that one," Matill said quickly. She took Sir Geoffrey some bread soaked in juice from the hare roasting over the fire.

The third man did not stir.

Afterward Pearl lay, wrapped in her cloak, staring up through the branches of a chestnut tree. Though Joan had insisted that Jack was dazed and had taken no notice of her, Pearl was sure that he had. She turned and sobbed quietly into her cloak.

FIFTEEN

SIR GEOFFREY

IT WAS a restless night. Those who slept at all slept fitfully. Widsith spelled Joan so she could rest, but he had been forced to call her back several times. Jack Bowman needed something more for his pain. Sir Geoffrey had tried to sit up and started bleeding again. Then the third man had roused himself and begun flailing about.

Shortly before dawn, Will took over. At daybreak Joan struggled out of the warmth of her cloak. Matill put a mug of hot cider in her hands and made her sit and drink it. Pearl brought some bread she had warmed in the embers.

"I think a change has come over them," Will told Joan. "Sir Geoffrey and Jack even spoke to me. They remember what happened. And I told them where they are." Glumly he added, "Jack recognized me from the day Rob smacked him."

Joan sighed and got up. She gave her mug to Pearl and walked wearily toward the wagon.

"Well, that settles it!" Matill said. "The rest of you go on. Rob and I will leave right now with Pearl. We will wait for you at Greencastle."

"And find yourselves dying in a ditch like these," Widsith said, waving toward the wagon. "Two women and a man alone on the road? How long before you came upon safe companions? Nay, Matill, there's too much danger in that."

Matill opened her mouth to argue, closed it again. Widsith seldom set himself against her, but it was clear he meant to have his way now. She shrugged and looked helplessly at Pearl.

As for Pearl, a cold numbness had come over her. The will to fight was gone. She could see that all along this was meant to be. Some way or other she was fated to be returned to Sir Geoffrey. Well, let him take her. She would struggle no more. Hot tears burned her eyes.

Through them she saw Rob watching her, silent and distressed. She went to him.

"I'll run away again, Rob," she promised. "Now that I know the towns you play, I will find you. Dear Rob, I'll be a trouper or die with the trying!"

He held her, making soft sounds deep in his throat.

They reached Wallbrooke at midday. As soon as the gatekeeper learned their business he sent a runner to the sheriff's house, another to clear the way for the wagon.

The unusual commotion brought gawkers from all directions to stand and watch, wide-eyed and openmouthed, as the troupe marched down the street behind the wagon.

The sheriff was waiting for them in front of his house. He had already sent a rider to the manor to bring the news of Sir

Geoffrey and to fetch the manor physician. Now he watched his men carry the wounded inside.

"Someone should see to them," the sheriff said. "If Sir Geoffrey should die before . . ."

"I will stay," Joan said.

When she would have moved to go with the sheriff, Widsith held her back. "Be you mad?" he demanded in a low tone. "Do you stay, then we all must stay. And what of Pearl? Let's get away from here, now!"

"Wait," Pearl said. "Joan is right. She can't leave those men now. Gwen will take us in. Come to us there, Joan, when you are done."

Joan nodded. She turned and hurried toward the waiting sheriff.

Matill hissed through her teeth. "That girl has more heart than head," she grumbled. "That be your failing, too, Pearl."

The reunion with Gwen was not the joyous one Pearl had dreamed of so often. She wept in Gwen's arms as Matill explained what had happened.

"My dear, you are not lost to us yet," Gwen soothed. She led Pearl to a bench and sat beside her. To Widsith, who had slumped down onto the weaving stool, she said, "You will all stay with me. There is sleeping room upstairs and I've plenty to eat."

"And you've plenty to feed," Matill said. "Pearl and I will help you with supper."

They ate late, after waiting in vain for Joan's return. Finally the men went upstairs to bed. Matill and Gwen sat with Pearl through the long night.

Early in the morning someone knocked at Gwen's door. Gwen

answered, expecting Joan. It was a messenger from Sir Geoffrey, come for Pearl.

"You'll not go alone," Widsith said firmly. He went with her, and waited for her outside the sheriff's house.

Inside, Pearl stood blinking in the darkness after the walk in the bright sunlight. There was a long table under the windows. Benches stood along one wall. Along the other, the wounded men lay on pallets. Sir Geoffrey and Jack Bowman were propped against pillows, freshly bandaged, looking almost cheerful. Joan bent over the still form of the other man.

Sir Geoffrey motioned Pearl to come near. "I can never recall the faces of all my serfs," he said, "but Jack says you are Big Rollin's girl."

Jack snorted, then winced with pain. "Aye, I've found you out at last! I saw you here, there, the other place, all the time wondering why you looked familiar. Girl, you sassed me once!"

"Where is your brother?" Sir Geoffrey demanded.

"I—I don't know, my lord," she stammered.

"Don't know, or won't tell?"

She did not reply.

"A good flogging will make her tell," Jack said.

Ignoring Jack, Pearl gave Sir Geoffrey a level stare. "You may have me flogged, my lord, and I may tell you something. But it will not be the truth."

Again the bowman snorted.

Pearl continued, her eyes on Sir Geoffrey. "My brother works in a town for his freedom. He'll have it before long now. That's the law!" Her voice broke. She bit her lip.

Sir Geoffrey gave her a curious stare. "So you know something of the law. What do you know of the laws of chivalry?"

The odd question confused her. She thought for a moment before replying. "I have heard of chivalry, my lord. It has to do with knights and ladies, I think."

He explained: "According to the laws of chivalry, whoever saves a life owns that life. Your friend Joan Lightfoot, here, has told me how it is that we owe our lives to you. But for you, she could not have used her skills on us. We'd have died, she says; but now we will live. Even poor Perry, my park keeper." He slumped back onto his pillows and groaned.

"Sir Geoffrey," Joan cautioned, coming to make him lie back on the pallet, "you will undo all I have done unless you take care. You promised your physician that you would do as I say or I cannot stay."

He groaned again. "I'll be as quick as can be," he promised. "Pearl Rollins, we are all three in your debt. Ask me for anything, and it is yours!"

Pearl's eyes widened. She hesitated; glanced at Joan, who smiled and nodded; then dropped to her knees. "My—my lord, I beg only to be free!"

He gave a short laugh. "Then you ought to have let us die by the roadside, for then you would have been truly free! Oh, we hunted you for a handful of days, then thought some wild beast had devoured you. 'Twas good riddance, I thought, since you were of such rebellious mind."

Her astonishment grew. She stood up, gaping at Jack Bowman. "But, he—your bowman—"

Jack chortled. "You thought I was chasing you? Hah! I remembered you only this morning. No wonder you skittered away when I tried to touch you that day at Reading Fair!"

"Jack was on an errand for me," Sir Geoffrey said. "He was to find me some good leather. I wanted the best, for my wife's new saddle."

Pearl's jaw dropped. All those terrible months of worry, and for nothing! And now she had trapped herself. Oh, why had she not listened to Matill?

Sir Geoffrey interrupted her thoughts. "So now I have you," he said. The words cut deep into her heart. "But I cannot keep you. Your kindness and courage have broken your bonds. Pearl, you have earned your freedom."

She tried to speak, and could not. She knelt to kiss his hand.

He said gruffly, "Go tell the sheriff I want ink, quill, and parchment."

Pearl found the sheriff in the small back room where he slept and took his meals. He gave her his writing box.

Over Joan's protests, Sir Geoffrey insisted on being led to the table, where he sat and wrote in large, black scrawls on a piece of the parchment. Then he rolled it slowly and handed it to Pearl.

"This is yours," he said. "I'll write another for your brother. Gavin, is it? You are serfs no more!"

Pearl stood stiff and unbelieving while Sir Geoffrey wrote out Gavin's parchment. When it was finished, she helped Joan bring him back to his pallet. The effort had cost him dearly. He was in great pain.

"God bless you, sir!" Pearl whispered. "And speed your recovery." She looked at the scrolls in her hand. If only she could read those magic words! What would Gavin say?

And Widsith! She had forgotten poor Widsith, pacing up and

down the street, waiting to learn her fate—and Joan's. She started for the door, then turned and stood uncertainly, wondering if she was dismissed.

Sir Geoffrey's smile was half grimace. "Farewell, and God-speed, Pearl Rollins."

Jack Bowman's pale face darkened in a scowl. "Best to stay clear of me, girl. You'll not get off so easily next time I ask you to share a flask with me!"

Joan went outside with her. "Tell Matill I must stay a few more days. Somehow Sir Geoffrey thinks Perry Parker will die if I leave too soon! But he has come round and will be sitting up tomorrow, I think."

She smiled and waved at Widsith, who had stopped his pacing and come running toward them.

When Pearl and Widsith reached Gwen's, they saw Barden in the yard and Wat's wagon nearby. Chop barked them a welcome as Wat opened the door to them.

"Pearl!" Wat cried, folding her into his strong arms. "See, Gwen, I told you Widsith would bring her back safely!"

"Nay," corrected Widsith, "Pearl brings *me* back, and with the best of news!"

Pearl turned in Wat's arms, but before she could speak Garth leaped onto her neck, nearly choking her. Rob moved to pluck him off.

"Let him be," Pearl said, laughing through her tears. "I thought never to see this old monkey again, so just let him be!"

SIXTEEN

GAVIN'S CHOICE

SO THEY WERE in Wallbrooke for the market days
after all. They had gathered at Gwen's to say farewell when
Joan arrived. Matill was sitting at the table counting money.

Joan stood in the kitchen doorway looking pale and tired,
but wearing a wide grin.

"Joan must have good news," Widsith said. "I say Jack Bowman has asked to marry her!"

Joan laughed. "Better than that," she said. She drew a pouch
from under her skirt and tossed it onto the table next to Matill's
money box. It landed with a clank.

"What's this?" demanded Matill.

Joan loosened the drawstring and turned the pouch upside
down. A rush of coins spilled out. She spread them on the table
for all to see. Then one by one she picked them up and returned
them to the pouch, which she held out to Matill.

Matill refused it. "Your nursing skill has earned you this. We agreed only to share what comes from trouping."

"Take it," Joan said. "We have *all* earned it. We have risked much and gained much these past days."

Matill accepted the pouch. "Even Mule has earned a share, I suppose, since he carried those fellows here." She grinned, and everyone laughed. She took some coins from the pouch and gave half to Wat, half to Gwen.

"For your welcome of us—and for giving us Pearl." Her words made Pearl's sudden new happiness complete.

Then it was farewell again to these friends, with hugs and tears and promises to return next year. They waved back at Gwen and Wat until they turned the corner.

Now that Pearl's fears were gone, she approached each new town with happy expectancy. At night she went to sleep imagining Gavin's face when she gave him his scroll.

They arrived in Bristol the day before the fair, and went directly to the pork butcher's for Gavin.

"Not here," the pork butcher said. "My nephew has come to stay with me. As you see, it needs only one boy to wash down this place."

"Then where?" demanded Widsith.

The pork butcher shrugged. "Who's to know? Have I the time to follow chance workers about?"

"Never mind," Matill said as they turned away. "So he is gone from this place. We will find him at another."

They walked down to the wharf, peering into shops along the way. A ship was in. A steward bawled out orders as men hustled into the vessel and staggered back out under the weight of chests and barrels.

Suddenly Pearl pointed. "I see him! Gavin!" She would have run to him, but Will held her back.

"Wait till he's done, else he'll earn a beating."

But Gavin had seen her. He grinned and waved.

They went on to the fairground, knowing Gavin would look for them there. Supper was nearly ready when he came. He had grown tall, and he was thin. But his eyes sparkled in his tanned face. He told them of his past year.

"Now I have work nearly every day," he finished. "I sleep with some others in a shed on the wharf. 'Tis not such a bad life! I've made friends with a cooper who makes ship's barrels. He will apprentice me when I'm of age."

Pearl had been scarcely able to wait to tell him *her* story. "And so we are free!" she said, showing him his scroll. "Now you can come with us to see Lady Hythe. We think she wants us all in her household."

To her dismay, Gavin was completely unimpressed by the scroll. "I'll keep this pretty piece of parchment, but I have no need of it," he said. "In less than a week I'll be a year and a day in Bristol, doing gainful work. I have earned my own freedom! And, Pearl, this life well suits me!"

She could not persuade him to come with them. Will, again, took Gavin's part. To Pearl's surprise, so did Widsith. Even Rob, in his silent way, showed his approval of Gavin's decision.

Matill sighed. "Let be, since he wants it, Pearl. We will see him next time we come through Bristol."

Finally Pearl gave up.

From Bristol it was not far to Swindon. They found the manor house and waited restlessly in the great hall, wondering if Lady Hythe would even remember them.

Off one side of the hall there were rooms hidden by curtained doorways. Along the other wall tables and benches were stacked, ready to be set up at mealtimes. At the far end of the hall was a table on a dais, where Lady Hythe sat at meals with special guests.

Presently they heard footsteps on the stone floor. The curtains parted at one of the doorways. Lady Hythe beckoned them into the room.

"Good day, and welcome!" she greeted them. She took the only chair, and signaled them to sit down. Pearl and Joan sat on low stools near her. Matill chose the window seat. The men crouched on their heels. Garth clung to Rob's neck, silent for once.

"You have come because I promised you a performance," Lady Hythe began. "Now I will tell you that it is for Prince Edward and his wife, the Lady Eleanor."

They exchanged startled glances. The prince!

Lady Hythe seemed pleased with the effect of her announcement. "However, there is more to it than that," she continued. "In the spring the prince will leave to join the new Crusade. With him go Lady Eleanor and others of his household—as I would have gone with my own dear husband, were I not needed here to manage his affairs."

No one moved. She had their whole attention. "The Lady Eleanor is my good friend, and I wish to give her a very special token of our friendship. I ask that your fine troupe accompany her on this dangerous journey, to bring her and the prince what pleasure you can."

Again she studied their faces. "You wonder why I have chosen you. First of all, when I saw you perform so beautifully I knew you would please my lady. But more than that, I like the way you work together and look out for one another. Such a generous spirit will serve you well, and the royal household, too, in what are sure to be difficult times."

She fixed her eyes on Matill's. "Not the least, it pleases me to see women among you. I think this will also please the Lady Eleanor." She stood up. They scrambled to their feet, each of them as mute as Rob.

"I will pay you well and provide for all your needs," she said. "But here is something else you should know. You will be years away in distant lands, where disease is as deadly as war! Should you decide not to take this risk, I will understand. Meanwhile, the prince arrives early next month, so prepare to entertain him. And know that you are welcome guests in this house."

There was a long silence after she left them. It was broken by a shriek from Joan. "The gypsy! Remember what she said about Pearl and a king? Prince Edward will be king of England one day!"

She flushed and glanced quickly at Widsith. "The gypsy also said that I would lose my love."

Widsith's unhesitating reply made the flush deepen. "No need to believe *everything* a gypsy tells you, Joan."

Matill tapped her toe on the stone floor, impatient to have the most important matter settled. "What are everyone's thoughts on this? Who says we stay? Who says we go?"

Each waited for the others to speak.

"I say we go," Widsith answered at last.

"Aye," said Will. Joan and Rob nodded.

"Then we go," Pearl said softly. She tapped Garth's head gently, making him nod. "Garth says we go, too!" Suddenly the tension eased. Everyone laughed.

There was a commotion out in the hall. Pearl drew aside the curtain to look. Servants were setting up the tables and benches. The rich aroma of roasting meat and garlic drifted from beyond the dais.

Helsa hurried toward them, her arms outstretched to Pearl. She wore a white apron over her blue dress, and a white coverchief over her hair.

"Helsa!" Pearl grunted in Helsa's fierce embrace.

Helsa laughed, releasing her. She included the rest in her smile. "You have come to play for the prince, I hear!"

They nodded, smiling. Then Helsa said, "Come, I will show you where to sit at table. Then I must get back to the kitchen. I can join you when the pies are done."

The servants opened the outside doors. People rushed into the hall, all talking at once. The dogs came, too, to sprawl under the tables and wait for scraps. Helsa led the way to the end of the second row of tables.

As they sat down, Pearl looked across the well-scrubbed surface at Matill. "I'm near starved, yet my stomach whirls like one of Will's rings," she said. "Here we are, all ready to go on Crusade with the prince. And for all we know, he'll not even want us!"

SEVENTEEN

THE PRINCE

THE FOLLOWING DAYS were busy ones. Lady Hythe employed a dozen seamstresses to make new clothes for the troupe: tunics of blue and white, yellow and red, over long green hose; short red capes with hoods. Even Garth had one.

They practiced, stood for fittings, practiced some more, and chatted nervously and without end about whether they would please the prince and his lady.

Widsith begged permission to go to London to see Fa Roger. Lady Hythe gave him leave, and a horse to ride. He returned, greatly saddened, with the news that the old man had died in his sleep one midsummer's night.

A few days later the prince and Lady Eleanor arrived. Resolutely the troupe put aside their grief. Fa Roger would not want them to give a melancholy performance.

The fateful evening came. They paced the small room off the hall, waiting for supper to end. Lady Hythe had sent Helsa to

keep up their spirits. "More like to keep us from running off," Matill grumbled, chewing on her fingernails.

A sudden loud blare of trumpets made them jump. A herald announced that there was a surprise prepared for the royal guests. Helsa pulled back the curtain.

"Now!" she commanded.

Obediently, Matill and Widsith marched out to face the long rows of guests sitting at tables now cleared of food. They were soon playing their merriest tunes, to the stomping of feet and the clapping of hands.

They changed tempo suddenly, to Will's juggling music. Helsa pushed Will out into the hall.

He halted, then strode to the front of the dais, tossing his rings and sticks. Pearl squinted, afraid he would miss and bring

everything down on his head. But Will's fingers were as quick as ever, his eyes as sure.

The prince, sitting next to Lady Hythe in the place of honor, led the applause. He was dark and handsome and sat taller than any man present. Longshanks, Pearl remembered folk called him.

The Lady Eleanor, slim and lovely, sat on the other side of Lady Hythe. She seemed delighted with Will. She clapped her hands and turned to say something to her hostess.

Matill was playing Joan's melody, now. Joan stepped through the curtain just as Widsith took up the tune. There was scarcely a sound but that of her feet and her dress and the music. Cheers and shouts filled the hall when she finished.

Next it was Rob's turn. A rope had been strung from end to end of the hall, over the space between the two rows of tables.

All held their breath as Rob began his walk. Pearl had never seen him do so well.

Then it was Pearl herself, and Garth. She rubbed her sweaty palms on her new tunic. Realizing in horror what she had done, she looked to inspect the damage. There was none.

"Go, and Godspeed!" Helsa whispered, pushing her toward the curtain. "And, Pearl! My lady says she will keep an eye on Gavin whilst you go on Crusade."

Pearl hugged her quickly. She crossed herself and spat sideways for luck. Holding Garth tightly, she stepped out into the crowded hall.

There was a stool for her at the foot of the dais. She hurried to it and sat down quickly, with an anxious glance at Lady Hythe, who nodded encouragement.

Pearl balanced her harp on her knees. With one final swallow and a whispered word to Garth, she began. To her great relief, Garth danced without fuss or flaw. They were not halfway through the song when she knew he had caught the fancy of everyone present.

Pearl strummed a final chord. Garth bowed low toward the dais, as she had recently taught him to do, before Rob crept out and whisked him away, to renewed applause. The dogs, stirred awake by the noise, added their yowls to the din.

Pearl rose and bowed, too. Then she reseated herself and ran her fingers over the harp strings. Instantly the room grew still, expectant. Gathering all of her courage, she looked directly up at Lady Eleanor and sang in her high, clear voice:

> "Let us sing of bright morn breaking
> From the glorious east;

Lilies fair their sheaths forsaking;
Larks in light their music making;
Sing the song of wings and waking
    That befits our feast!

"Apple boughs in white are dressing,
    And in heaven's wide blue arch
Little clouds, like angels pressing
    Rank on rank with cheeks caressing,
Shed their softness like a blessing
    On our joyful march!"

Tears filled Lady Eleanor's eyes. Pearl knew she had under-
stood the reason for this song on this night. It was Pearl's own
prayer for blessings on Lady Eleanor's coming journey with her
husband.

Again the response was wild and loud. But now Lady Eleanor
stood up and beckoned Pearl to come forward. The prince had
risen, too, and this brought everyone to their feet. Pearl walked
stiff-legged and trembling up the dais steps.

They like us! Her heart sang the words as she clutched her harp
with tight, damp fingers and bowed low before the royal couple.

Lady Hythe had sent for the others, and now they came march-
ing out from behind the curtain to take their share of the praise.

Pearl watched proudly as Lady Hythe presented them to Prince
Edward and Lady Eleanor. These friends had brought her far
and done much for her. Now she would not fear to sail to the
farthest places with them—nor even to walk ashore in the midst
of the warring Turks and Christians!

AFTERWORD

PRINCE EDWARD joined a Crusade in the summer of 1270. The following year he won a great victory at a place called Haifa. Not long after this, his father, the king, died, and the prince became King Edward I of England. He returned home four years after this story ends.

F
VAN

C'

Van Woerkom, Dorothy

Pearl in the egg